Alina took a deep breath and exhaled slowly.

"Try this on for size. Ryan Erikson is not a stranger to me. We dated in college. No...not just dated. We were serious. Engaged. And I haven't seen him since we said good-bye just before graduation."

Deidre's face drained of color. "Until he came to Flash?"

"Exactly. You saw him last week before I did. Back then Ryan was devastated with the breakup. I hurt him terribly, and then I sank into severe depression." She stared into her glass of water, still seeing the hurt look in Ryan's eyes when she'd told him they couldn't be together. "I heard he ended up in counseling, but I don't know that for sure."

"Did you break up on bad terms? No closure? If that's too personal, I understand."

"Deidre, I broke off the relationship. I was frightened about the future. I had Anna's care to consider, and the prospect of taking on a husband overwhelmed me." Alina dug her fingers into her palm before reaching for the glass of water. "Other things were involved, too. Things I don't want to discuss, but it meant leaving Ryan behind."

"I'm sorry. And to think you have to work with him for the next three months." Deidre took a sip of her iced tea. "Do you think he still has feelings for you?"

"I have no idea." Her pulse raced.

Deidre gasped and leaned closer across the table. "Do you have feelings for him?"

Leave it to Deidre to home in on what really bothered her. "That's a moot point."

DIANN MILLS lives in Houston, Texas, with her husband, Dean. They have four adult sons. She wrote from the time she could hold a pencil, but not seriously until God made it clear that she should write for Him. After three years of serious writing, her first book, *Rehoboth*, won favorite **Heartsong Presents** historical for 1998. Other publishing credits include magazine articles and short stories, devotionals, poetry, and internal writing for her church. She is an active church choir member, leads a ladies' Bible study, and is a church librarian.

Books by DiAnn Mills

HEARTSONG PRESENTS

Don't miss out on any of our super romances. Write to us at the following address for information on our newest releases and club information.

Heartsong Presents Readers' Service
PO Box 721
Uhrichsville, OH 44683

Or visit www.heartsongpresents.com

Flash Flood

DiAnn Mills

Heartsong Presents

This book is dedicated to my sister Debbie, who always finds the sunshine in the rain.

A note from the Author:
I love to hear from my readers! You may correspond with me by writing:

DiAnn Mills
Author Relations
PO Box 721
Uhrichsville, OH 44683

ISBN 1-59310-794-3

FLASH FLOOD

Our mission is to publish and distribute inspirational products offering exceptional value and biblical encouragement to the masses.

All of the characters and events in this book are fictitious. Any resemblance to actual persons, living or dead, or to actual events is purely coincidental.

All scripture quotations, unless otherwise indicated, are taken from the HOLY BIBLE, NEW INTERNATIONAL VERSION®. NIV®. Copyright © 1973, 1978, 1984 by International Bible Society. Used by permission of Zondervan Publishing House. All rights reserved.

PRINTED IN THE U.S.A.

one

"Excuse me, could you repeat that?" Beads of perspiration dotted Alina Marlow's face. Her heart pounded in her ears, and her stomach did a wild twist. Surely she misunderstood the announcement. She moistened her lips and peered into her boss's face.

Fred Lineman, owner of Flash Communications, rose from his leather executive chair. He cleared his throat and coughed, the telltale sign of his heavy smoking days. Lines in his tanned face, which Alina hadn't noticed before, were the characteristics of a weathered old man. Granted, he'd experienced some health issues, but when had this happened?

"Alina, and the rest of you," he said, glancing around the paneled boardroom, "I know this comes as quite a shock, and I assure you my decision did not come without a good deal of deliberation, many sleepless nights, and much prayer. I'd like to explain the buyout in more detail." He reached for the pitcher and poured a glass of water. His hand trembled.

Alina observed his uncharacteristic behavior, but the questions blaring across her mind demanded answers. "Why weren't we informed of this earlier?" The moment the words left her mouth, she regretted her selfish attitude. Fred needed support from his leadership team, not criticism from a key member.

"Because there was nothing any of you could do." Fred set the glass on the table. His pallor alarmed her, especially with his recent heart attack and his failure to lose any substantial amount of weight. "For some time now, the residents and business owners here in Radisen have pressed me to expand our services to include such things as high-definition TV, high-speed Internet, voice services, and home security. You've heard their complaints and requests just as I have. We've sat in this very room and discussed each issue. Several months ago, I began to investigate our options and resigned myself to the facts at hand. I had to either make a major investment into Flash or find a company that could better serve our customers. In addition, my doctor and my wife are insisting I retire." He glanced around the boardroom, briefly making eye contact with every employee present. "We are a small-town business. Even if retirement wasn't in the picture, I'd need to do what's best for our customers. This means a buyout from Neon Interchange, a global company equipped with the latest technology."

"What does Neon's buyout mean for us?" asked James Ferguson, the installation foreman. Since James was known for defending his men and having a quick temper, his reddened face came as no surprise.

Alina shifted in her chair. *James, don't lose it. I want to know what this means for me, too.*

"I'm not completely sure what the takeover will entail, but on Friday you'll have the opportunity to pose your questions to Neon's regional director. He and I will be working in a closed session tomorrow through Thursday to discuss the details and procedures."

"When will Neon officially take over?" Alina swallowed hard. *I can't lose control of my emotions here.*

The older man looked grim, and why not? He'd started Flash Communications in his garage and watched it grow into a viable business. His chest rose and fell with a deep sigh. "I'd estimate about three months. You'll know more at Friday morning's meeting."

"Will we lose our jobs?" asked Deidre Blackman, Alina's dear friend and secretary.

"It's possible some of you might need to seek different employment." Fred's concerned gaze swept around the room as though he spoke to family.

James tossed his pencil across the mahogany table. "Great. Radisen is certainly not known as a hub of job opportunities, unless you want to take to fishing on the Ohio River."

"I'm sorry, folks," Fred said. "I'm not happy about this either. What I want you to understand is that this didn't come easy for me." He gathered up the file folder before him. "Please save the rest of your questions until the meeting on Friday. I want to give you accurate information." He nodded and left the meeting—a first for the otherwise personable owner of Flash Communications, who never left the boardroom before his employees.

Two sealed boxes of donuts sat in the middle of the table. Full pitchers of water and two decanters of the finest coffee hadn't been touched. Stunned, Alina allowed Fred's announcement to settle into her brain. The frustration she'd tried to mask at the beginning of the meeting now surfaced to a near boil. How could he spring this news on them without some type of warning? He'd always been open and honest about the company's dealings. Board meetings were a time to toss around ideas, discuss customers' problems, and brainstorm about how to better serve the community. As a solid Christian, Fred began each session with prayer for guidance and wisdom. Obviously he'd elected to forgo any direction with this decision. A man of God—a good shepherd—took care of his people; he didn't shove them out of their livelihood.

Alina willed herself to calm down. Anger and misguided thoughts didn't solve a thing. She heard the others grumbling but didn't want to discuss any of the new information with them, especially with her frenzied emotions. Besides, none of them had answers—only questions ushered in by all the fears involved with a potential job loss. No doubt they all felt betrayed, like she did. The big guns had won again; advanced technology and more money to buy out the smaller companies had the advantage.

Alina heard her name, and she peered up into Deidre's tiny face. Of Vietnamese and American descent, Deidre possessed tremendous beauty. But her inward beauty came from a deep love for the Lord and those around her. Of all the staff, Deidre held the trophy for true employee loyalty: ever faithful, always kind, and full of optimism. Right now, Alina didn't want to hear any generous statements about Neon Interchange or Flash Communications, neither did she want to be placated into thinking all was right with the world.

"I'm a little upset right now." Alina shook her head. If only she could dispel the doubts and worries plaguing her mind.

Deidre touched her arm. "I understand. When you're ready, we can talk. This will work out; wait and see."

Alina bit back a nasty remark. Deidre didn't deserve a dose of Alina's wrath, and neither did Fred. "There has to be a solution. The idea of looking for another job petrifies me. And I wonder what I'd do without a paycheck to support Anna."

"If I say God will provide a way, it will only upset you." Deidre toyed with her watch, then gathered up her laptop.

"I'm sorry. I know you and Clay have your parents to support—along with providing for your children. You, of all people, understand how critical this is. I'm not doubting God; I simply wish He'd warn us about setbacks."

Deidre nodded. "This is a stretch for my faith, too." She raised her shoulders and smiled. "I have brothers and sisters to help with my parents' care. Anna just has you."

Alina would make sure Deidre had a box of chocolates and a bouquet of daisies on her desk before the day ended, along with a note of apology. Friends didn't treat friends without love and respect.

Thoughts of Alina's mentally challenged twin sister raced through her mind. She'd taken on the financial burden of Anna's care since high school days when her mother's limited income failed to support the expensive facility, and Alina didn't take her responsibility lightly. The concerns weren't about herself; she'd find another job and get by. But with the possibility of her losing her job and of her sweet sister no longer obtaining excellent medical care. . .

I'm second in command here. There's no danger of me losing my job. I'm important to this company. Fred tells me so all the time. I need to relax. I'm overreacting.

With an air of determination, Alina powered down her laptop and left the boardroom. Whether Fred wanted to talk or not, she intended to discuss this ludicrous idea. She could pick up the slack, and he could cut his work hours in half. She'd make it work. She knew how.

Fred's closed office door should have deterred her, but Alina needed answers before Friday. Company protocol stood in second place when it came to friendship. She had to offer assistance and find a way to save Flash from the hard tactics of big business.

Confrontation is healthy medicine. Clears the air and gets rid of the junk that smells. This will work out.

Ignoring Fred's secretary, she knocked lightly on his door and stepped inside without waiting for permission. Closing the door behind her, Alina drew in a sharp breath. Fred's face was buried in his hands, while his Bible lay open on his desk. The impulse to leave him to his privacy nudged at her spirit, but she simply couldn't. Not today. Not this issue.

"Alina." He failed to look up. "My door is closed. That means no one is to interrupt me."

"I have an idea." Her voice shook, ripping apart her confidence.

"Believe me. I've played out every scenario imaginable. I have to retire, and I have to sell Flash."

"But, Fred—"

"What part of 'Do not disturb' do you not understand?"

His sharp response startled her. "I'm sorry, Fred, but I can't leave until I have a few answers."

He stared up into her face. Weariness cemented lines in his face, leaving no doubt as to his sixty-three years. "I don't have any more to say than you've already heard. Now please leave me alone."

Still holding on to the laptop cradled in her arms, she braved forward. "I believe you haven't worked through all the options. I think you're hiding something from the rest of us. This isn't fair. We could have helped with a solution."

Fred's fist pounded against his desk. "Never, Alina, never in all the years I have known you have I ever stated that you were out of line. Flash Communications is my business, and what I do with it isn't your concern. You, above everyone here, should know how I feel about this company."

The words stung. Fred and his wife, Marta, had been like parents to her. They'd shared holidays, company outings, church pews, prayer requests, and countless hours riding horses on their property. Still, the need to have matters resolved propelled her into the questions jarring her senses. "Why do we have to let a global company come in and take over things? We're handling our customers just fine by ourselves."

Silence—and the scent of Fred's old-fashioned lime aftershave—wafted around the room. She waited, not moving from her stance near the door or slipping into a chair in front of his mammoth wooden desk. The laptop in her arms felt heavy, cumbersome.

"We are *not* properly taking care of our customers. We don't have the capital to spend on a new infrastructure that is necessary to deliver the expanded services our customers are demanding and deserve. With Neon's money and expertise, Flash will be able to provide the latest technology available in the industry." His voice rose, and the creases in his forehead deepened. "Alone, it would take us years of increasing our rates to recoup the money required for such an upgrade to our network. The economy is such that the banks just won't go out on a limb and loan us the necessary funds. None of this touches on what my work schedule is doing to my health. My wife deserves to have a husband during her retirement instead of spending her old age as a widow."

At last she understood. Fred had no choice. Selling Flash was killing him as much as it tormented her. The realization caused her to choke back sobs. *I'm so selfish. All I'm thinking about is my own problems.* "I apologize," she whispered. "I've been wallowing in self-pity over the buyout and forgetting what this company really means to you."

"Alina, I sincerely don't know who will have a job and who won't."

"Of course." She reached for the doorknob. "I'll save the rest of my questions for Friday. I'm really sorry." Without another word, she left the room and walked down the hall to her office. *Neon Interchange. I hope they're not out to bleed the life out of everyone here. I'm scared, really scared.*

The people of Radisen had gotten along just fine without all the extras. Why start now? They were a small town with good country folk as customers. A rash of new indignation surged through her body. She wanted to tell every one of those citizens that their demands had forced a family-owned business into a buyout—and placed a wonderful man's health at risk. Fred's work schedule resembled the hours of two men half his age. He knew every facet of the business and had the customers' files memorized. His tireless work in the community—from volunteering his time and money, making donations to worthwhile charities, and visiting shut-ins at the hospital on Sunday afternoon—was a part of Fred Lineman.

Alina wanted to fix it all. The thought of her friends losing their source of income made her ill. Maybe if they all supported Fred and demonstrated optimism, Neon might decide to keep them all. For starters, she'd send a mass e-mail to all the employees urging them to work together as a team.

She stopped at Deidre's desk. "I'm springing for lunch today—for everyone in the office. Order out for pizza. I refuse to allow bad attitudes to spread in here like poison ivy."

"Your discussion with Fred must have paid off."

"Not exactly. I've been hit with a case of guilt for my insensitive response to Fred. He deserves better than my sarcasm—even if I don't end up with a job."

two

Once Alina left work for the day, she drove to visit Anna in the picturesque facility for the mentally challenged. The drive to the home, nestled in southern Ohio, featured winding roads lined with oak and pine trees. She munched on a grilled chicken sandwich and fries while she enjoyed the passing scenery. The setting always relaxed her and took the spin off the day's hectic pace, but this evening was especially hard. She tried to relax her hold on the steering wheel while envisioning spring wildflowers in the weeks ahead instead of the snow that was piling up at the sides of the road. *March—in like a lion, out like a lamb*, drifted across her mind.

She pressed the window button and let the cool air bathe her face. *Freeing* best described the sensation, as though all her troubles had vanished. No longer was she Alina Marlow, business executive, sometimes sharp and sometimes temperamental, the woman who worked overtime without pay and battled servicemen to fill work orders. Here, whizzing down the road with the wind blowing back her hair, she almost believed her world had been liberated from problems.

A sign indicating the turnoff for Homeward Hills prompted Alina to take a right. She reached for the stuffed rabbit on the seat beside her. Anna loved soft things. She'd cuddle them to her cheek and giggle. Sweet Anna. . . Her oblivion to reality seemed like a blessing. Anna had not progressed since the date of her accident when the girls were three years old. In many ways she'd digressed even younger, and childhood toys and treats pleased her the most.

A few moments later, Alina parked her car in the visitor area and snatched up Anna's rabbit. A chill wrapped around her with the sun settling into the west, and she pulled her coat tighter. All of the day's happenings suddenly washed over her like threatening storm clouds. Spring was supposed to be the season of hope and the anticipation of new life, but not this year, not with Neon taking over Flash Communications. For the moment, Alina felt reasonably secure in her job. *I'm practically indispensable.* She cringed at the thought. How futile.

At times like these, she envied those who lived inside the rustic-looking facility, without the bothersome worries plaguing the rest of the world. The lodge effect, with the abundance of trees, gave comfort to those who had loved ones dwelling there.

The elderly receptionist inside Homeward Hills greeted Alina by name. "Your sister is in the group room."

"Thanks. I'll find her." At the entrance of the huge area designated for games and visitation, Alina stood in the doorway and watched a staff member feed her sister applesauce. In addition to her obvious mental challenges, Anna spent her waking hours in a wheelchair and was slowly going blind in her left eye.

Her dark-haired twin made laughing sounds. Anna's speech lacked many words, but Alina had learned to distinguish what many of her sister's vocalizations meant. At first, she didn't want to disrupt her sister's snack. Anna looked serene, almost radiant in her childlike mannerisms. The top and sides of her long, wavy hair, thick like Alina's, had been brushed back and captured in a ponytail. Anna glanced up, and a wide smile spread across her face.

Alina strode across the room and embraced the joy of her existence. "Hey, pretty girl," she said. "I'm so glad to see you."

Anna giggled, then turned to the attendant and opened her mouth for another bite of applesauce.

"I'd like to feed her," Alina said.

The attendant nodded and kissed the top of Anna's head before relinquishing the plastic spoon to Alina. Her sister's eyes widened, and she attempted to clap her hands. Alina pulled a chair next to her sister. "Oh, my sweet, sweet girl. I love you so much."

⁊ₐ

Tuesday, 7:45 a.m.

Every Tuesday morning at Flash began with a Bible study before work. Alina had never known Fred to miss one, until today. Once again the boardroom filled with employees, but the normal hum and laughter had vanished since yesterday's session. Donuts sat untouched on the table. Perhaps these were left over from yesterday.

"I think I'll pass on Bible study." James reached for the coffee. "Not into it today."

Alina searched for words to encourage and persuade the man. "I'm not in the mood either. I don't think any of us are, except now is the time when we do need to delve into God's Word."

James crossed his arms over his thick chest. "Who's leading it? You?"

Before Alina could answer, Deidre cleared her throat. "Fred phoned me last night and asked me to take over this morning," she said. "And since I didn't have time to prepare, I thought we'd read Psalm 139 and do prayer requests."

"They'd all be the same request," James said.

"Maybe so." Deidre poured a cup of coffee and opened the donut box. "And if that's the case, we can all pray for each other."

Most of the group stayed, except James and a woman from accounting.

"I understand how they feel," Alina said a few moments later, "because I'm angry, too. The idea of praying for the Neon executive with Fred makes me physically ill. He's charting our future, and we're nothing more than names and numbers." She took a deep breath. "But I will do what pleases God—and pray my attitude improves."

"I caught a glimpse of him in Fred's office," Deidre said. "He didn't look like the enemy."

"Satan never does."

&

Friday, 8:00 a.m.

Alina thought she'd burst before Friday's meeting with the executive from Neon Interchange. Fred and Mr. In-Charge had met somewhere away from Flash for the past three days, which thoroughly infuriated her. She wanted to size up this fellow and make her own observations before the meeting. In truth, she wanted an opportunity to corner him about a few pertinent matters—like job stability for herself and the others.

"Thirty minutes until the meeting." Deidre plopped down a cream-filled buttermilk donut and black coffee on Alina's cluttered desk.

"You're a doll." Alina watched the steam rise from the granite blue cup with Flash Communications' logo stamped on the side. Oh, how she needed the extra caffeine this morning. "You know I can't resist coffee and a good donut."

Deidre grinned. "I thought about bringing you stroganoff from last night's dinner, but Clay ate it all before going to bed."

"My kind of guy." Alina licked a dollop of chocolate cream filling from the corner of her mouth. Guilt suddenly assailed her, and she laid the donut on a napkin. "Listen, Deidre, I've been a real bear this week."

"Understandably so," her friend replied. "This has been rough on all of us."

"No excuse. I apologize for every time I've been short and totally out of line. Please forgive me. That's not the way friends treat each other, and I claim to be a Christian."

"It's okay, really." Deidre smiled. "Besides, it made for interesting conversation around the dinner table. Clay couldn't wait to hear the next episode with all the juicy details."

Alina nearly rose from her chair. "You what?"

"I'm teasing." Deidre laughed and pushed back her shoulder-length black hair. "But I had you going."

"Only for a minute." Alina shook her head. "I was beginning

to detest myself. Unfortunately, my resolve to improve my attitude hasn't been successful."

"A few more minutes and you'll have some answers."

Alina gripped the coffee cup. "Not so sure I want to hear Neon's plans, but since my job is on the line, I'll be firing questions and comments left and right."

"Nothing new there." Deidre glanced through the window to the outer office area. "There's Fred, and I recognize the man from Tuesday morning. Come see for yourself. Both are smiling. Good sign."

Alina moved to the doorway to catch a glimpse of the two men. She shivered, and a moan escaped her lips. *No. This can't be happening.* "There must be a mistake." *Ryan Erikson.*

☙

Ryan knew he'd have to face Alina sooner or later. He preferred later. When he learned she worked for Flash Communications and was the key person to assist him through the transition, he wanted to resign and take the first flight out to some desolate place in northern Russia. At the sight of her, the past six years vanished and the old tug at his heart pounded out his longing. Her dark hair, tucked professionally behind her ears, and her glowing complexion were reminders of her love for the outdoors. Instantly he found himself propelled back to another time, and his emotions surfaced. Striking as ever. She lifted her chin. Challenging as ever. He caught her attention, and even from a distance, he felt the coldness. The idea of battling her bitterness over this takeover left a vile taste in his mouth. He remembered her stubbornness and the pent-up little girl inside. He also remembered the good times between them. Someday he'd confront her as to why she broke off their relationship. But not today.

Today he'd present Neon's business arrangement to the employees of Flash Communications and hope none of them followed him back to his hotel. Their jobs were in jeopardy, their lives about to be altered. All of the training Neon Interchange had provided still didn't prevent the sinking feeling he experienced when he had to break unpleasant news—and do so with professionalism. He didn't dare let them see how he ached for those who would lose their jobs. How many times had a wife or husband phoned and begged him to reconsider? He could do little but pray for those affected by job loss.

"Thanks for paving the way for me," Ryan said to Fred. "That makes my job a little easier."

"They've had a few days to digest the buyout," Fred said. "I know you've done this type of thing before, but as I said yesterday, these folks are more like family than employees."

"From what little bit I know of you, I wouldn't expect anything less."

Fred expelled a heavy sigh. "And from what I know about you, I can see you're going to do everything possible to help them through the transition."

"Business negotiations are one thing." As they moved closer to the meeting area, Ryan sensed the growing hostility. "But a heartless executive is never what I want to be."

"I explained the reasons for the change, but I know some didn't hear a word I said." He greeted a young woman as she passed by. "For me, retirement is something I've considered since my heart attack. I feel a mixture of responsibility to these folks and my love for my family. I'm selfish, too. I want all of them to be happy and to make a good living. Christian ethics play a major role, too."

"I wish every situation like this one had a Christian in charge. Sure makes it easier to work through the process."

"Well, there is obstacle number one, my right-hand lady, Alina Marlow," Fred said. "Highly qualified, like a daughter to me, and very hurt about this buyout. I haven't had the time to talk to her like I wanted, but she knows it's inevitable. The sooner you soothe her concerns, the sooner the rest of the employees will follow her leadership."

"I'll do my best."

Fred ushered the way into a small boardroom where water

and coffee had been set in the middle of the table. The room held an icy blast.

"Feels like someone has the AC on instead of the heat." Fred frowned. "Sure hope that wasn't done on purpose."

Ryan chuckled. "Wouldn't be the first time. We might as well get started."

He watched the employees of Flash Communications file into the room and seat themselves around a large rectangular table. Extra chairs lined the far end of the room, against the wood-paneled wall. Silence—the usual greeting—grated against his nerves. The employees appeared frightened, and a few looked downright hostile. He'd feel the same in their shoes.

Fred stood, and the room quieted. "Folks, this is Ryan Erikson from Neon Interchange." Fred's bearing demanded attention. "He is in charge of communications between Flash and his company, and he is the director of the transition process. As you already know, for the past few days Ryan and I have been talking about the best way to complete this transition. I've grown to appreciate his professionalism and call him a friend. I am counting on you for cooperation and giving 100 percent of your abilities, just as you've always done for me."

Ryan took his place beside Fred and shook his hand. He waited while the former owner of Flash sat down beside Alina, knowing the formal courtesy showed his and Neon's utmost respect for the company's owner.

"I imagine most of you are filled with questions about what this buyout means to you. I'm here to provide answers to the best of my ability. Neon Interchange wants to make this transition as smooth as possible. We understand your need to keep your jobs and your desire to avoid any unpleasantness during the next three months. Eliminating positions is not our goal, but effective and economical business practices are our focal point.

"Our goal is to provide this great community with the service and technology of larger metropolitan cities. These services will include high-definition TV, additional channels, wireless Internet, security monitoring, and computer-integrated telephone systems. Neon has the capital to upgrade the hardware and software necessary to bring these services to Radisen. In advance, we'll bring in a team who will train you on how to use the new technology prior to deployment. This way you'll be prepared to answer customers' questions and solve any problems related to the new services.

"In addition, employee benefits will exceed those already in place here at Flash Communications. As Neon Interchange employees, you'll have access to new dental and vision plans, plus improved medical programs to choose from. Neon also has a great profit-sharing program and a 401(k) with company matching funds up to 6 percent of your gross wages, as well as other retirement benefits.

"We're all on the same team now, and I look forward to getting to know each of you as we progress through this three-month transition period. I'd be happy to answer your questions now."

A man lifted his hand. "My name is James Ferguson. I'm the installation foreman. How many of our jobs will be eliminated?"

Ryan nodded. "Good question, and I wish I had the answer this morning. We've already identified some positions that will no longer be necessary or will be filled by Neon personnel out of necessity. Those employees affected will be notified privately as soon as possible. Other positions in question will be evaluated over the next several weeks."

"Will you be doing the evaluation and deciding who stays and who is booted out?" James asked.

"I will be making the recommendations; however, the final decision rests with Neon."

"How special." James narrowed his eyes and shot Ryan a venomous glance. "How soon will we know?"

"Depends on the job and how quickly we all work through the transition. Quality service personnel are needed regardless of the buyout. You and I will talk privately about your team of installers and their qualifications." The mixture of fearful and angry looks he received tugged at Ryan's conscience, but he'd long since been schooled in keeping a professional demeanor.

An Asian woman wiped a tear from her eye; she was Deidre Blackman, the secretary he'd seen at the desk outside Alina's office.

"Neon does offer a severance package for key individuals. I will have that information available for those affected in writing next week. What is important to remember is to continue your jobs as always. Fred or I will notify you if something changes."

"What about relocation?" a young man asked.

"That is also a possibility."

"To Columbus?" Alina asked—her first verbal communication since Ryan opened the meeting to questions. She sat back in her chair as though she were in charge. How well he knew her facade, especially when she wanted to cover her emotions.

"Not necessarily. We have offices around the country and in Canada, Germany, and Denmark. If a position is available, any of you are invited to apply."

"If we want to discuss this transition with you privately, is there a problem?" The sarcasm lacing Alina's words were grim reminders of the past.

"No problem. I understand Deidre Blackman will be assigned to me during this time, and anyone who wishes to see me can make an appointment with her." He nodded at Deidre and smiled. "She and I have time scheduled right after lunch to go over procedures and establish when those appointments should be made."

"Deidre is my secretary," Alina said.

Whoa. Got her riled now. "Let's talk right after this meeting. I won't have too many things for her, and I think we can both utilize her abilities without overworking her in the process."

Alina said nothing, but he had a strong feeling their meeting would be reminiscent of their college days just prior to graduation.

"Where is your office?" James asked.

"I will be sharing space with Alina Marlow." From the corner of his eye, he saw her stiffen. Fred should have told her about the arrangement, and for a moment he felt sorry for her. Everything about this takeover had to be tough. "If there are no more questions, I'd like to turn this meeting back over to Fred." Ryan paused, and when no one spoke he added, "Thank you for your attention, and I appreciate your cooperation."

Fred clasped his hand on Ryan's shoulder before addressing the group. "I'd like to thank all of you for your attendance. None of this is easy, but I'm counting on you to support Ryan. I, too, am available to discuss the buyout and help with the transition in any way I can." As he spoke, the owner of Flash Communications projected the same confidence that Ryan had seen over the past few days. "I'd like to end this meeting with a personal request. Let's show Neon Interchange why and how Flash Communications has been successful here in Radisen, and let's work together to give our customers the expanded services they've been asking for. Thank you." When Fred stepped aside, the employees stood and began working their way toward the door.

Now was the time for Ryan and Alina to talk about her involvement in the days ahead and Deidre's role. He'd rather face the rest of the employees in a dark alley.

three

Alina smiled at her friends and waited until they left the boardroom before making eye contact with Ryan. She trembled and proceeded to put each chair around the rectangular table in place. Talking to Ryan was harder than she'd ever imagined. The relationship they'd shared ended abruptly—harshly. And she'd been the one to break it off.

His gaze captured hers, and he smiled, but she couldn't return the pleasantry. Not yet. She'd gather the strength in a few minutes and hope Ryan couldn't see how his presence affected her. The memory of his pale blue eyes had haunted her for years, and the sight of his wheat-colored hair reminded her of how she used to tease him about the color being bottle-blond. In reality, he'd descended from Scandinavia. Both of his parents were fair. . . . *Don't go there.*

Ryan hadn't changed much, except in the way he chose his words. She recognized the keen intellect, and she saw something else, too—a warmth and peace not there in years gone by. Everything about him emanated political correctness; he was the epitome of an executive. He still possessed the same compassion and caring in the way he related to people—even more so. She had always appreciated those special qualities about him, despite the action she'd taken.

"Alina, are you ready to talk now?" Ryan asked.

That same question echoed from the past when she'd refused to discuss why she'd broken off their engagement. "Yes, I'm ready. Where did you have in mind. . .to discuss things?"

"Use this room," Fred said. "I have things to do." He turned to Ryan. "I appreciate your treatment of the situation."

She rolled Fred's words around in her head. Did "treatment of the situation" mean she'd lost the fight for her job before it began?

"No problem. I'll head your way once Alina and I are finished," Ryan said.

Fred sent Alina a sincere smile, and she did her best to silently convey reassurance that she would not sabotage Flash Communications. The door closed, seeming more like a final assessment of Fred's company than an opportunity to discuss the future with Ryan.

I'm such a cynic. Ryan has forgotten about me by now. Our past has nothing to do with my work here. She glanced at his left hand to see if he wore a ring. Nothing. She didn't know whether to be relieved or not. In the next thought, she realized his unmarried status was not a good thing.

"Shall we sit down?" Ryan asked. "I have a list of things to go over, and I want to take whatever time we need for each one before I talk to Fred and Deidre."

Alina pulled out a chair she'd just replaced. Opening her notebook to a new page, she finally made eye contact. For a moment, she saw a hint of sadness in his eyes; then it vanished. In its place was the look of a man who had nothing more than business on his mind. She dug her fingernails into her palm.

He opened his laptop and powered it up. "I want to keep track of our discussion, then e-mail it to you later. That way we're on the same page."

Her thoughts scrambled back to when her insides felt like jelly at the sound of his voice, much the way she felt now, but for a different reason.

"I'm curious as to why you'll be sharing office space with me," she said.

"I'm told it's large enough to accommodate both of us, and it makes sense since we'll be working together for the next three months."

"During the entire transition?"

He nodded. "Alina, this may be hard, but I'm sure we can

put aside our past personal life and work for the good of the company. Being friends is important to me."

"You forget one important factor. I don't agree with this buyout."

"I understand, but neither one of us was a part of that decision." His shoulders lifted and fell. "Do you think I chose this assignment?"

"I have no idea." But it would be a grand way to execute revenge for breaking off their engagement. She shook her head. The past needed to stay there.

"I've never been vindictive, and I don't plan to start now." He paused. "All that aside, how are you?"

"All things considered. . .I'm fine."

"I don't see a ring, so I gather you aren't married."

Strange that he noticed. "No. Just Anna and me."

"How is she?"

"Happy. I have her in a wonderful facility near here."

"I'd like to see her."

Please, Ryan. "That's probably not a good idea. She was attached to you."

His smile stayed intact. "I understand. You're probably right. Shall we get started?"

Relief caused her to slowly expel a breath. "I really need to know what my responsibilities are for the next three months."

"We'll go through each customer's file to evaluate their current service and see how Neon can better serve them. I have software that we'll use to merge data and complete reports. Financial reports along with employee information will also need to be done."

Alina laid her pen beside the notepad and placed her hands in her lap. He wouldn't see her nervousness if she hid her shaking hands. "Does Neon have a position for me after the transition is complete?"

She read no emotion in his gaze, and it bothered her. Up until this moment, he'd been the Ryan she remembered, carefully choosing his words. Unless. . .

"That's why I wanted to meet with you first thing this morning," Ryan said.

Her stomach knotted. "I won't have a job when the transition's finished, right?" A chill swept through her body. A state of powerlessness gripped her senses.

"I'm afraid so. You won't have a position with Neon," he said. "An experienced management team will arrive and assume responsibility near the end of the transition period."

An ache crept into her heart. "I'm supposed to help you make a smooth transition, cooperate in all facets of this buyout, and in return I'm relieved of my job? That's a wonderful thank-you."

"Neon has many opportunities in locations all over the country for someone with your abilities. I work out of Silicon Valley in California."

Why does he have to act so calm? "It is impossible for me to relocate with Anna." She stood and gathered up her laptop, purse, and notepad. "Get someone else to help you. I'd rather quit or get fired."

"By staying you'll receive a good severance."

The silence between them seemed to punctuate his words. She had no choice. Ryan knew it. She blinked and attempted to swallow her hostility. "Whatever happened to being rewarded for company loyalty and business ethics? Do you and Fred think that letting people go will make Neon a better organization?"

"Fred has nothing to do with this. He cares about you very much and has a tremendous amount of respect for what you've done with Flash. It's unfortunate, I agree. I will be glad to write you a letter of recommendation when our work is finished, possibly sooner."

Bribery. "You know I have no choice." She meant to cover the caustic emotions but failed.

"We always have a choice."

Was he referring to what she did six years ago? She could not, would not discuss it. "All right, Ryan. You win. And I'll take you up on that letter of recommendation. When do we begin?"

"Tuesday morning. I'll move into your office later on this afternoon. I have to be at the Columbus office on Monday."

"Are you taking my desk, or do I get to work at my own?" She realized her words were laced with venom, but she couldn't help it.

Ryan peered out the window, then back to her. "I have a question for you. Would you talk to any other executive the way you're speaking to me? I understand that our differences and our history play into all of this, but I don't appreciate your hostility."

Alina clenched her fists to stop her reaction to his words. "My hostility? What about my livelihood? I could use a little sensitivity here."

"What do you suggest? I could have sent you a memo about your position or have the home office mail you a certified letter in about two months. But that isn't the way Neon or I conduct business."

The sting hit Alina as sharply as if Ryan had slapped her. She'd have preferred it. "You're right, and I'm sorry."

&

Friday, 5:45 p.m.

Alina managed to work the rest of the day without another serious encounter with Ryan. She'd behaved horribly this morning—nothing short of crass—and the memory of it twisted at her insides. She should have asked about his family and thanked him for asking about Anna. She should have plastered a smile on her face and offered her utmost cooperation. Instead she made a fool of herself.

Strange, Ryan asked to see Anna after all this time. But he'd always been good with her.

Once at her townhouse, Alina kicked off her shoes and brewed a cup of peach herbal tea. Normally she made decaf coffee on chilly evenings, but tonight she needed to fill herself with something healthful—maybe it would counteract the poison she'd spewed at Ryan. A part of her wanted to call him and make sure the working relationship was all right. Anger toward Neon nudged at her, but she'd have to hide it.

While the peach tea lingered in her senses, her mind spun, and she moved from room to room, adjusting drapes, running her finger along the moisture on the windowsills, and staring out into the darkening shadows. From her bedroom, she studied a beech tree outside her window. Years ago, Ryan had carved their initials into a tree just like this. They'd been at a park when he declared his love. In his exuberance, he made sure their initials would last for eternity in the smooth bark of the tree. They were juniors in college then. Odd, she recalled her camel-colored wool coat and the red hat and scarf she wore that day. And she could picture Ryan in his leather jacket that always seemed to capture his cologne. Yes, she remembered it too well.

As the evening wore on, Alina found it difficult to concentrate on anything. Tomorrow she'd see Anna. The gloom of winter still threatened the days, but Anna loved to be outdoors. As long as there was no ice, Alina could push Anna's wheelchair into the patio area.

Finally she gave in to the overwhelming urge to relive her past with Ryan. On the top shelf of her closet sat a cardboard box filled with memorabilia from her college days. She stared at it for a long time before retrieving it. Once the box rested in her arms, she blew off the dust and carried it to her bed. Alina hesitated. Would this be like opening Pandora's box? Surely not. She'd kept these things to remind her of a gentle man, a beautiful love. Pressing her lips tightly together, she lifted the lid.

Dried yellow mums lay strewn across a mound of treasures and frosted the memories of each festive occasion. Alina read little notes and sweet cards that made her laugh and cry—each one tugging at her heart and filling her with regret for the stance she had taken. A purple giraffe reminded her of a carnival and stolen kisses on a Ferris wheel. A playbill from *Phantom of the Opera* brought back her twentieth birthday.

They'd passed on dinner because the tickets had cost so much. Movie stubs. Napkins. A small heart-shaped candy box. She picked up a photograph taken of them with friends. They were blissfully in love then. . .but it wouldn't have lasted.

Yes, she had opened Pandora's box.

four

Ryan yawned then groaned as he glanced at the clock on his nightstand. Friday had been a long day, brimming with antagonism from some of Flash Communications' employees. He'd had a deep, sinking feeling that Alina and the installation foreman, James Ferguson, had planned a get-together, and it wouldn't be pleasant. James had cornered him Friday evening when both men left Flash at the same time.

"Neon needs to know what it's like to be on the receiving end of bad news," James had said.

"I understand your frustration."

Two women from the office staff walked by and echoed "Good night" to the two men.

As soon as they passed, James lifted a brow. "Better watch out. Your uppity nose might get broke before this is all over. Good people don't like losing their jobs."

"I know how to be careful, and I don't appreciate being threatened." Ryan had been down this road before.

"I'm not threatening anybody. I'm merely making an observation. Besides, it looks to me like Neon's taking advantage of a sick old man."

Ryan shook his head and walked away. Too many tempers had erupted today, and he wasn't in the mood to play into the hands of one more disgruntled employee.

Now, as Ryan lay awake, he stared at the ceiling and relived the entire day. A nightmare had awakened him—the second one tonight dealing with Flash Communications. His subconscious must be working overtime. This time a contract on his life had Ryan on the run while picketers from Flash walked around his hotel carrying protest signs. Alina and James led the group. *I've been doing this too long.* The thought of all those people at Flash planning his demise made his cold hotel room appear cozy.

He loved weaving other companies into Neon's conglomerate. The process compared to a puzzle, and he found immense satisfaction in making sure the pieces fit. Yet downsizing employees left a nasty taste in his mouth. If left to Ryan, none of those people would lose their jobs, but no one at Neon ever asked how he felt.

His thoughts shifted to a career question for which he had no answer. A possible promotion had been mentioned before he took the assignment in Radisen: a vice president position in Columbus, no travel, and a substantial pay increase. Yet Ryan dragged his feet, and he really didn't know why. His family lived there. . .old friends. . .roots. A picture of Alina filled his mind.

Memories of college days moved to the forefront of his mind, especially those times when he'd teased Alina about her many causes: everything from saving trees to women's rights. Then he learned about her twin sister, Anna. Together they visited the mentally challenged girl. And together they paid regular calls to Alina and Anna's widowed mother, a peculiar sort of woman who, in Ryan's opinion, criticized Alina far too often. Amid the family dysfunction, he saw Alina's heart and fell in love with her. If she hadn't broken the engagement, he'd be married to her today and not reminiscing about the love left behind.

Odd, how the sound of Alina's voice still moved him to think about spending the rest of his life with her—although on Friday, she evidently had an impenetrable wall built around her. If they'd had closure and she'd explained why the relationship wouldn't work, he might not feel this old pull at his heart. No one had ever taken Alina's place. She had tried to return the engagement ring, but he couldn't bring himself to take it.

He'd tried for years to forget her and thought he'd put it all behind him until yesterday. The problems between them could have been worked out, if only he'd known the source of them. Ryan allowed the sadness and regret to wash over him until a twinge of anger took their place.

Another man might enjoy the irony of it all. She'd treated him badly, and now he could seek his revenge by relieving her of her employ. Ryan found no satisfaction in that arrangement. Perhaps while working side by side with her over the next three months, he'd find out why she broke off their relationship. Ryan saw her heart for Flash Communications' employees; she was a real crusader. Their needs were important to her. No doubt, she'd fight him all the way to day ninety over the transition. He expected no less. *My Joan of Arc.*

Finally sleep enveloped his thoughts and pulled him from his reflections about Alina. Ryan welcomed the rest, for he'd wrestled with the same questions for far too long.

ã

Saturday, 8:00 p.m.

Working in the hotel room, Ryan realized his stomach shouted for dinner. He'd been so busy putting together correspondence to Neon that time had slipped right by. Shoving back from his desk, he contemplated where he could get a good meal on a Saturday night without waiting an hour for a table.

"I should have gotten something to go earlier," he said to the computer screen. Traveling had driven him to the eccentric level, or he'd officially become his father since he was talking to himself, giving voice to the older man's admonitions.

He tucked in his shirt, ran a comb through his hair, and snatched up his cell phone, wallet, a book about living life as a Christian man, and his keys. Maybe he needed larger pockets or a purse. He chuckled. Now he'd become his mother: He was laughing at his own jokes.

After conferring with the young woman at the hotel desk for restaurant recommendations and receiving no help, Ryan drove his SUV to a popular chain restaurant. As he expected, the wait for a table was forty-five minutes, unless he wanted to sit at the bar. The hostess handed him a beeper, and he slid onto a bench outside the building with his book. An evening chill whipped about him, but he detested the noise inside while reading. *What Happens When the Past Becomes the Present.* *That should be a good chapter, one I could have written.* The subtitle indicated the problems that occurred when a Christian man faced what he'd done as a non-Christian. Oh yeah, he needed this chapter in a bad way. He immersed his attention in the book—until he heard his name.

"Well, look who's here," the familiar, hostile voice said. James Ferguson, the foreman at Flash, planted his feet in front of Ryan.

Ryan glanced up, pausing briefly at the hole just above the knee of a pair of dirty jeans. His gaze trailed up to the man's smirk. "Hey, James. Good evening."

James chewed on a wad of gum. "It had the makings of a good one until you got here."

I'm not in the mood for this. Ryan turned his attention back to the book.

"I'm talking to you."

Ryan closed his book. What had he read in the last ten minutes that might help him with this angry man standing before him? He stared down at the rough surface of the walkway and prayed for guidance. God loved James the same as He did for Ryan. So what should he say to lower James's hot temper while displaying strength and not weakness? Running sounded like the easy way out, but sooner or later Ryan had to deal with James and settle the matter between them.

"I'm talking to you." James's voice inched up a notch.

"I heard you. What kind of response were you expecting?" Their gazes met. Ryan had encountered hostility before, but not this openly.

"Respect, for starters."

"Respect? You insulted me, James."

"I don't give respect to people who put my friends out of work."

"Look, I have a job to do at Flash, just like you. People other than you and me made decisions, and we're involved with the result. Plain and simple. I don't want to argue or toss barbs back and forth."

"Sorry, I can't help myself. The sight of you makes me see folks out of work with families to feed. I don't get a warm feeling from that. Whether it's me or not ain't important. It's the principle of the thing."

Ryan sensed his own irritation gathering momentum. "What do you want me to do?"

"Pack up and leave. We who care about Fred can get this thing turned around with Flash. No one needs a big company running our business." James spat on the sidewalk.

"Sorry, James. I'm staying. We have to work together, like it or not."

James's eyes widened. "Want to take this to the parking lot? I'd love the chance to tear into you—break that nose of yours."

Ryan stood from the bench, his finger holding his place in the book. "I'm not leaving my job here, and I'm not fighting you. If my presence bothers you that much, I'll go to another restaurant." He refused to get baited into a sophomoric mentality, and he refused to sacrifice his integrity. If James chose to flatten him, the man could sit in jail, because Ryan wouldn't hesitate to press charges.

"You're afraid of me."

Ryan nearly laughed at the irony; it was James who was frightened. Instead he shook his head. "No, I'm not. You don't want to make a spectacle of yourself in front of all these people waiting for a table, do you? Aren't you a family man?"

"Glad to hear you're so concerned about others. When did that happen?"

Ryan turned and walked toward his vehicle. He'd have drive-through for his dinner tonight.

"This isn't over yet," James said. "Some of us are talking.

You'd better be keeping an eye out, because we're waiting."

Ryan whirled around and retraced his steps until he faced James squarely. "I suggest you think before you speak, James. Do you need a reminder about who is making the recommendations for job placements?"

Without waiting for James to reply, he made his way to his vehicle and cast his focus on a hamburger and French fries for dinner.

five

"I invited Ryan to church, but I don't see him." Fred craned his neck toward the parking lot.

Alina glanced around them in the hope that neither Fred nor Marta saw her discomfort.

"What's he look like?" Marta asked. She stood shoulder to shoulder with her tall husband.

"Blond, blue-eyed, muscular, and a nice smile," Alina said.

Marta threw her an odd look. "I thought you didn't care for him. Sounds to me like you listed potential boyfriend material."

Fred laughed. "My guess is it would snow in July before Alina entertained that thought."

Don't even go there, Fred. "I was being nice," Alina said. "You know, working on changing my attitude to display a show of respect and integrity."

"I bet you rehearsed that the whole time you were getting ready for church," Marta said. "Truthfully, I know this has been hard, and I praise your efforts."

"It's all God, because I'd like to run him out of town." Alina laughed at her absurd comment, then added, "I really am trying."

"Toss some of your good intentions James's way. He's really got it in for the guy," Fred said.

Alarm propelled through her veins. The last thing she wanted was to see Ryan on the receiving end of one of James's volatile outbursts. She'd heard about the foreman's temper, even seen it in action when one of the servicemen neglected to complete a job to James's satisfaction. "I hope James's animosity is all talk."

"Let's pray so. I keep telling myself any man who's a volunteer

35

fireman and comes to a Bible study can overcome his dark side." Fred scanned the parking lot one more time. "Ryan must have changed his mind. We best get inside before the service starts. I haven't seen James and his family either."

Alina admitted she wanted to go to church alone—without Ryan. A wicked thought, but the truth. Going through the box of keepsakes had left her feeling as though she'd been tackled by the old emotions. Sitting on the same pew with him would distract her from keeping her love for him separated from good sense—and the real reason for attending church. Worship needed her full attention.

"Are you coming?" Marta asked.

Alina swung a confused glance at Marta, then at Fred. "Where?"

"Church. Are you all right?" Marta asked.

"Sure. My mind was wandering."

Fred chuckled, and it irritated Alina. It irritated her very much.

Once inside the small red-brick church, Alina settled into the pew beside Marta and Fred. She glanced around at the familiar surroundings: the stained-glass windows that had been there since the church was built in 1928, the cross suspended from the ceiling, the organ on one side and the piano on the other. Each item represented importance to the Sunday worship, but the most important ingredients were the worshipers and God.

Tears streamed down her face as fast as she could whisk them away. Marta placed her hand atop hers, but Alina dare not look her way.

"Things will work out." Marta leaned toward her. "Fred has connections within the industry that can help you find another job."

Alina nodded, afraid to speak for fear she'd dissolve into a pool of tears. Her sweet friend believed the emotion stemmed from the upheaval at Flash, and perhaps that was best for now. But Alina knew her tears came from her relationship with Ryan. God wanted her to state the truth, but she couldn't do it—not now or ever. And the knowledge made her miserable. Granted, the situation at Flash had upset her, but she'd find another job. The circumstances between her and Ryan, though, wouldn't have a good ending. Once they completed the transition, he'd go back to his world, and she'd stumble back to hers. All she'd have left was a dusty box of memorabilia and more regrets than she had before.

God, please help me be strong. I keep making one mistake after another, and I'm not glorifying You. Help me to be You when I deal with Ryan. Is it possible to be his friend and not feel this horrible ache in my heart? I'm sorry for my caustic words. I really need You to guide me through this.

❧

Monday, 8:00 p.m.

Ryan sorted through the deluge of e-mail. One day of not checking his mailbox, and every member of Neon had to copy him on a post or request information. In addition, many of the personnel worked via e-mail on Sundays. Ryan vowed a long time ago to keep the Lord's Day free from work. Sometimes he traveled on Sundays, but he made it a point to avoid working— not to be legalistic but to show reverence for the day. He'd been invited to attend church with Fred and his wife yesterday, but he attended a different one to avoid Alina. He hadn't figured out if that decision was godly or not. When he'd thought about it long enough, he realized if his presence upset Alina, then it was best he stay away.

He continued to collect e-mails; the number pushed at the one hundred mark. *Nice to be needed, but today the idea of hibernation has a lot of merit. This onslaught of messages must be why I haven't dared take a vacation since I started working for Neon.* Today's meetings in Columbus had been routine except for a closed session with some of the top executives.

"We want to reiterate how much we want you as part of the team here in Columbus," the chairman of the board said. "You have the communication skills necessary to head up a division that would act as a liaison between the needs of the acquired smaller companies and the parent company. You're a great team player, an asset for any corporation. As a VP, you'd have very little travel and a substantial pay increase."

"I appreciate your offer, and I've been giving it a lot of thought," Ryan said. He should have said he'd been praying about the offer, but he refrained.

"We need an answer by mid-April. Although we don't want to look for another person to fill the position, we will need time if you choose not to accept the job."

Stress and pressure. Just what he needed on top of everything else clouding his mind. "I understand. If I accept, what happens with the transition at Flash?"

"You'd finish that assignment before assuming your new duties."

"You'll have my decision, possibly sooner than your deadline." Ryan weighed the pros and cons of the job. Mostly he came up with pros, and the cons were his insecurities about taking on more responsibilities. The bottom line was that God called the shots, and Ryan had no idea what He wanted.

He scrolled down through his e-mail, reading the messages that looked important, saving the others until later, and deleting the junk. His cell phone rang, and he snatched it up, eager for the diversion. Fred greeted him.

"Before I go to bed, I wanted to check in with you about our eight o'clock meeting," Fred said.

"Is there a problem?"

"Possibly. Flash always has a Tuesday morning Bible study for those who want to participate. It's at seven thirty and usually runs forty-five minutes."

"Why don't I join you?" Ryan chuckled. "After last Friday, being a part of a Bible study with the group who hates me might make the next three months a little easier."

"That bad, huh? I got wind of a few of the remarks, and I handled them from my end."

"Job security is a big issue, and I don't blame them for feeling hostile. I'd feel the same way. Anxiety has a way of bringing out the worst in people. It's the wanting to slit my throat that bothers me." Instantly Ryan regretted his words. "Hey, Fred, forget I said anything about Friday. Those folks have every right to their opinions. And I'm serious about attending the Bible study, unless you think it might make the others feel uncomfortable." *Like Satan tuning in for tips on how to make a believer's life miserable.*

"Fine, Ryan. I think it's a great idea. We're discussing First John, chapter three, verses eleven through twenty-four."

"Thanks. I'll read it beforehand. Would it help if I brought bagels or a fruit platter?"

Fred laughed. "I have the food part covered. Seriously, is James or Alina giving you trouble? I've discussed the situation with both of them, but I can again."

"Absolutely not. I've worked with men like James before. And I believe after the talk Alina and I had, we'll be able to work together without any serious issues. Fred, this is my job. Trust me in that I can handle situations that arise from the buyout."

"All right. But if anything comes up with any of my people, I'll talk to them. What I hope they realize is that Neon is not the enemy. The flip side of this is I could have closed down the business, and none of them would have a job."

"Unhappy employees happened to be my major in college." Ryan pushed his "happy" voice. "The work will get done in the allotted time. I'm sure they'll come to realize what you did is for their benefit as well as the customers'."

"But I won't have any of them causing problems on my watch. Good night, Ryan. See you in the morning."

Once the phone lay on his desk next to his car keys, Ryan opened his Bible to 1 John. He well knew the passage—all about loving each other. *"Let us not love with words or tongue but with actions and in truth."* He cringed. Some well-meaning person could easily use this verse to criticize Ryan's job of downsizing Flash Communications. He didn't plan to attend the Bible study to gain support for the transition; he always needed a fresh word from God. Ryan wondered if Alina embraced Christianity and if she would be there. They had attended church together a few times but never discussed the importance of God in their lives. Never lived it either. Going to church was more of "the thing to do" than the meaning of life. Another regret.

Ryan closed his laptop with the realization that his presence in the morning could make matters worse. The last thing he wanted at a Bible study was to open a can of VWMD—verbal weapons of mass destruction. So dare he go, or should he have his own quiet time with the Lord?

ತಿ

Tuesday, 8:15 a.m.

One more time Alina attempted to concentrate on Deidre's reflections on what it meant to love everyone despite your feelings about their actions and behavior. Alina's thoughts focused on Ryan, the same place they'd been since Friday. The Bible study this morning seemed to be directed at her. She'd treated him shamefully the last time they were together, and she needed to make amends with a sincere heart. An apology made for selfish reasons disappointed God.

This buyout wasn't Ryan's fault, and she had no right to blame him. He'd been right; if he'd been a stranger, she wouldn't have been rude and uncooperative. The details of the buyout had been decided long before Ryan came into the picture. At least this way, some of the employees would still have jobs, and the customers would receive exceptional service. She should be thankful for this decision—but it was one of the most difficult things she'd ever attempted.

Alina blinked several times in an effort to stay alert. Today she'd be working alongside Ryan. Today she hoped to have a new attitude. Today she'd feel all the tension of working with a man she once loved. The mere thought of those feelings gripped her heart. She reached for a cup of coffee in the hope that her brain would jump into overdrive. The merger and the three-month transition would be a whole lot easier if Ryan weren't in the picture. One look at him or the sound of his voice brought back the longing she thought she'd buried.

God, is there a good reason for this? I'm trying not to be selfish, cynical, and all those other things that take root in me. I want to honor You with all of me. Oh, Father, just seeing Ryan fills me with misery and thoughts of what I abandoned. I don't understand my own heart, but I know You do.

"I think too many of us fall under the category of loving with words and tongue and not in actions and truth," Deidre said. "When I read this last night, I thought of Ryan Erikson. I realized I'd been rude when I should have offered friendship and respect for his position." She pointed to Ryan. "Now here he is in our Bible study. And while I'm on a roll, I could have been much more encouraging to Fred. This merger is no one's fault. We've always said the customer comes first, and Neon will make sure their needs are met. So I want to say I'm sorry to both of these men for not living my faith. I wish everyone at Flash were here this morning so I could express my regrets. We've often spoken of how many need the Lord, and then we crawl into our own selfish worlds and do nothing to mirror the Lord. I pledge to show in my actions not only the love of Jesus, but loyalty to Flash and Neon."

The only sound in the boardroom came from the hum of the furnace.

Why couldn't I be transparent and state those godly things? Alina smiled at Deidre. She wanted to speak up and say how much she appreciated her dear friend, but the words refused to come. Perhaps Alina feared turning into a blubbering idiot.

"Thank you." Fred cleared his throat and coughed. He reached for his coffee. Deidre's candid statement had affected them all.

Ryan must have sensed everyone's attention on him. He nodded, stared down at the table, then fixed his gaze on Deidre. "I've worked through many buyouts and transition periods. Some have been smooth and pleasant. Others have been difficult. But I've never had a company allow me to attend a Bible study nor had anyone admit they harbored ill feelings and apologize in front of others. I appreciate your faith and your willingness to work through a situation in which you have no idea whether you will have a position at the end of three months. That takes guts and deep faith. Thank you, Deidre." He sat back in his chair and reached for a cinnamon roll. "I offered to bring bagels or a fruit platter this morning, but Fred was afraid I'd dip them in arsenic."

"Might eliminate a lot of headaches for you," Fred said with a grin.

Laughter rose, breaking the awkwardness. Alina wished she had Deidre's humility, Ryan's ability to lighten situations with a heavy dose of humor, and Fred's interest in others. Later she'd tell them how their words had touched her. Perhaps someday Alina could be a light instead of a candlesnuffer. She turned toward Ryan and trembled. Meeting his gaze, she mustered a smile. Did he have any idea how difficult her gesture of peace was? She committed to living her faith and exhibiting professionalism despite the fact she hadn't stopped loving Ryan Erikson. The truth held such pain that she felt physically ill. No one could ever learn the truth, most of all Ryan.

After the Bible study, Deidre, Ryan, Fred, and Alina discussed the goals and responsibilities for the transition team.

"The majority of the work will fall on Alina and Ryan," Fred said. "Deidre, you'll assist in however the two need your help. I'll continue to run Flash while feeding needed info to Ryan and Alina."

"Neon uses software technology that will allow integration of your files in a relatively easy manner," Ryan said. "I suspect we'll have everything converted to the new system in about six weeks. Once we make the switch, I'll need everyone on staff for the next six weeks to make sure the transition goes smoothly. Hitches are bound to occur, and these need to be worked out before I make my full report to my boss in Columbus."

"When will employee evaluations take place?" Alina asked, and Fred stiffened. "It's all right, Fred. I'm only asking for my own information—so I can plan." She shook her head. "I intend to do what I can for you. I apologize for my actions last week."

He offered a faint smile. "Glad to hear that. You're a pivotal person in this process. I need your expertise."

"I'll do my best."

"That's all I ask."

But I won't have a job. And I don't feel like being nice. This may be the best solution for Flash, but I don't see why God couldn't have done something different with me.

six

Tuesday, 12:15 p.m.

By lunchtime, Ryan and Alina had settled into somewhat of a working relationship. Their conversation teetered on the fence between formal and rehearsed. A wall, built from the rubble of miscommunication six years ago, seemed to stand between them. It left him frustrated, and yet he couldn't do a thing about it. The whole matter hammered into his control-oriented temperament. After Fred disappeared into his office and Deidre went to work at her desk outside Alina's door, Ryan could have split the tension in the room with an ax. Unfortunately, he was as much to blame as Alina.

He powered up his laptop and logged on to Neon's site, while the past stayed on the forefront of his mind. He wanted to talk about it, but instead he talked about software programs and what needed to be done first. They avoided eye contact, and their words sounded like verbiage from an employee manual. Conversation topics that centered on business emptied from his mind; he could only concentrate on the task at hand. He decided to focus on work and not on the woman beside him who smelled faintly of an exotic flower and looked entirely too appealing dressed in a spring green pantsuit.

Ryan cleared his throat, but words failed him—Ryan Erikson, the communications major who traveled around the country bridging the gap between small companies and Neon Interchange. What a joke—and one he planned to keep to himself.

Suddenly the date occurred to him. "It's Saint Patrick's Day," he said.

She lifted her head from the mound of files on her desk.

"What brought that up?"

"Your green suit."

She laughed just like she used to when they teased each other. Now, as then, it reminded him of a little girl running breathlessly in the wind. Odd, how he still felt the same analogy, the same lift in his spirit.

"Most of the women here today are wearing something green," she said.

"Guess none of them wanted to be pinched," he said. She lifted a brow, and immediately he realized what he'd said. *Great going.* First he couldn't think of the right thing to say, and now he'd made an inappropriate comment. *All I need is a harassment suit.* "Oh, that came out all wrong. I'm sorry."

Again she laughed. "You aren't wearing green, but I'll pass on the pinching."

"Nice of you to give me one concession. I'll hide in here for the rest of the day in case someone else notices."

"You'll get hungry." She pointed to her watch. "It's twelve thirty."

"I need a bodyguard."

"Sorry, the only one we have is the foreman."

Ryan winced. "And he hasn't decided if he likes me or not." Actually, James evidently had decided, but Ryan refused to bring up the subject.

"I imagine he's out looking for a pot of gold."

He could read a whole lot into her statement with the job situation there at Flash, but he chose to ignore it. "What about you? I'll spring for lunch, if you promise to keep the leprechauns away."

She hesitated, and he sensed the bantering had ended. "Is that such a good idea?"

"It's business, Alina, unless you've made other arrangements."

"Deidre and I have plans." She moistened her lips. Ryan inwardly smiled. Alina's gesture had not changed; he'd succeeded in triggering her nervous button. The realization gave him no satisfaction.

"I see." He forced a smile. "I'll see if Fred is in the mood to play bodyguard. What about dinner? I'll still need someone to protect me."

She tilted her head. Curiosity lit her cool brown gaze. "Why? It's been over six years."

"I'd simply like your company."

"It's not smart, Ryan. People might talk."

"I'm not out to make you feel uncomfortable or push you into something you don't want. All I asked was to take you to dinner. We're friends, and friends enjoy the company of each other. I'd like to hear what has been going on in your life."

"We're different, and there's no point in disguising it. Neither of us would be able to eat." She glanced down at her desk. "I can't, Ryan."

"No problem. If you change your mind, let me know." He pointed out the six-foot glass window separating her office from the hallway. "I see Fred. I'll corner him about lunch."

Without looking Alina's way, he headed for the door, longing for fresh air after nearly drowning in her presence. "Hey, Fred, how about some green chili to celebrate Saint Patrick's Day? I'm buying."

ᴥ

Tuesday, 1:00 p.m.

Talk to me," Deidre said. "Was the morning that bad with Ryan? I mean, I saw a difference in your attitude after Bible study."

Alina picked through her salad. She glanced down at it, forgetting what kind she'd ordered. *Chicken.* Exactly how she felt about telling her dear friend what was really bothering her.

"Are you worried about losing your job? I still can't imagine the company running without you. Why, you're a staple, like bread and milk."

Alina sighed and laid her fork alongside the plate. While she searched for words, she rested her hands in her lap. "Job security is part of it."

"Sweetie, trust God for your future. I imagine Neon will need you. I mean, next to Fred, you run Flash."

Alina shook her head. "I'm not indispensable. None of us are, no matter how much we think we're worth. Ryan told me my position will be eliminated after the transition is complete. Neon already has someone in line for what I do."

Deidre gasped. "I'm so sorry. With Anna's care and all, this has to be more difficult than any of us can imagine."

"It is, especially since I have to work with Ryan to ensure the process goes smoothly. And he did encourage me to apply for something at one of the other Neon offices."

"What do you think about that?"

"If not for Anna, I'd apply. Homeward Hills has been Anna's home for many years. They take excellent care of her and love her. They do a better job than I ever could." She — shook her head. "No, I can't consider relocating any farther than Columbus."

Deidre wrinkled her nose. "I'd have to pray hourly if it were me. I'll tape a reminder on my computer and my refrigerator to pray for you."

"Thanks, and I could also use a prayer to land a job. I'm not sure what Radisen can offer, and the idea of taking a cut in pay when my budget is already maxed out isn't good either. Well, let's just say I'm not looking forward to any of it. Like a naive child, I expected to work for Fred and Marta until I collected a social security check." Alina forced another smile. "But obviously God has another plan, and I keep telling myself it has to be better than any I could conceive."

"Will you start sending out résumés right away?"

"Oh yes. Tonight I'm going to take a look at my old one and search online to see how I can update it."

"Once you land a new job, I'm sure you'll feel more optimistic. One good point is you don't have to consider a husband or boyfriend in all this."

Alina shivered.

Deidre's smile vanished. Her dark, slanted eyes edged

downward. "What's wrong? Have you met someone and now your life is even more complicated?"

Alina looked out across the busy café. Amid the clatter of dishes, the smell of Italian food, and the buzz of voices, she listened for the Voice from above to give her direction. Too much of her life had been misguided, and she wanted desperately to stay in God's will.

"I hesitate to tell you this, because I don't want anyone else to know." She took a deep breath. "I am a private person to a fault."

"You know I can be trusted, but make sure what you are about to tell me is. . .a matter that you should tell me. I'm your best friend, Alina, and I want to help you any way I can."

"I know you are. My mind is racing with a problem I can't do a thing about. I'm trapped, more like petrified, and I need a friend to help me reason this out."

Deidre nodded. "You've helped me many times since we've become friends. Remember when I learned my parents needed to move in with us? You prayed with me and helped me garner the courage to talk to Clay. And remember when the doctor suspected birth defects with little Hadley? You were right there praying and supporting me. I'll do all I can."

"Okay." Alina took a deep breath and exhaled slowly. "Try this on for size. Ryan Erikson is not a stranger to me. We dated in college. No. . .not just dated. We were serious. Engaged. And I haven't seen him since we said good-bye just before graduation."

Deidre's face drained of color. "Until he came to Flash?"

"Exactly. You saw him last week before I did. Back then Ryan was devastated with the breakup. I hurt him terribly, and then I sank into severe depression." She stared into her glass of water, still seeing the hurt look in Ryan's eyes when she'd told him they couldn't be together. "I heard he ended up in counseling, but I don't know that for sure."

"Did you break up on bad terms? No closure? If that's too personal, I understand."

"Deidre, I broke off the relationship. I was frightened about the future. I had Anna's care to consider, and the prospect of taking on a husband overwhelmed me." Alina dug her fingers into her palm before reaching for the glass of water. "Other things were involved, too. Things I don't want to discuss, but it meant leaving Ryan behind."

"I'm sorry. And to think you have to work with him for the next three months." Deidre took a sip of her iced tea. "Do you think he still has feelings for you?"

"I have no idea." Her pulse raced.

Deidre gasped and leaned closer across the table. "Do you have feelings for him?"

Leave it to Deidre to home in on what really bothered her. "That's a moot point."

Deidre peered into Alina's face.

"Can't get much worse than this, can it?" Alina shrugged. "If I had a better sense of humor, I'd say the situation was comical, even movie material. I vowed never to see the man again. I had to go on. Then six years later, he shows up where I work. I'm assigned to help him during the transition of a buyout and work side by side as though nothing ever happened between us. He believes we can put aside the past for the good of the companies. Then he tells me I don't have a job after three months." Alina again reached for her water glass. "I'm not being fair. Ryan is a very compassionate man. He didn't enjoy giving me that tidbit of information at all. You know, they say confession is good for the soul. Why don't I feel any better?"

"If this wasn't so incredibly sad, I'd offer chocolate."

"Don't bother. I'd eat the whole box and have nothing to wear." She looked into her dear friend's face. "Any advice?"

"None, except I don't think your feelings for him are a moot point."

Alina moistened her lips. "Let's table that discussion."

"I already know the answer."

The waitress walked by, and Alina asked for a to-go box. Maybe she could eat the salad for dinner. "It is comforting to know Ryan's a believer. Neither of us had pledged our lives to God back then. I hope you understand that telling you about him is probably one of the toughest things I've ever done."

"You have my confidence. I wish I could do more than listen."

Guilt born of self-centeredness attacked Alina, leaving a queasy feeling in the pit of her stomach. "I haven't asked how you're faring in this mess."

"I'm fine. If I need to look for employment, Clay can handle the bills for a while. No problem." She paused. "Is it possible for someone else to work with Ryan? Could I take over?"

"No. Already tried that approach. Besides, Fred asked me to cooperate, and I gave my word. He and Marta mean too much for me to take a selfish stand, and I will not tell either of them about my history with Ryan."

"Fred might be more understanding than you think."

"The fact remains that Fred needs to retire, and Flash needs Neon's expertise for our customers. I know I argued that things were fine, but sooner or later another cable company would put themselves in a position to give better service. Anyway, none of those things matter. I have no choice." Alina pressed her lips together. "Let's change the subject, because there are no solutions to the myriad of problems surrounding Ryan and me in our past personal and present business relationship." She pressed her fingertips against her temples. "I'd cry, but it wouldn't solve a thing. At least I'm fairly certain life can't get much worse."

&

Tuesday, 7:00 p.m.

Ryan stepped into his hotel room. His suite boasted high-speed Internet with a large desk, an upscale kitchenette, a separate living area, a king-size bed, a bath he could have shared with three other guys, and other upgraded amenities. Despite all these conveniences, loneliness had crept over him the moment he left Flash Communications.

Although his job required solitude and a lot of travel, tonight, weariness settled on him more than usual. Over dinner this evening at a less than best restaurant—a tasteless yet colorful meal consisting of baked chicken with a leatherlike coating of cheese, a spinach and lettuce salad with partly frozen tomatoes, and rolls hard enough to level pins in a bowling alley—he toyed with the idea of the promotion in Columbus. At least there he knew where to get a good meal. He could have handled tonight's food a whole lot more easily if Alina had consented to join him. Perhaps she'd been right. Why put himself through the misery of missing her company?

Yet the idea of phoning her lingered. He could claim it was for business reasons and ask her a few questions or clarify something about today. The idea of asking her to work overtime one night this week when she might be more agreeable to sharing dinner with him wiggled through his mind. Ryan slammed his fist into his palm. Alina would see right through that ploy. She had no desire to be with him; she as much as said so today. He shouldn't call, wouldn't call.

He thought about her mother and wondered if they had mended their ragged relationship. Since Alina did not open up easily, he doubted things had changed. He used to believe her mother was the deciding factor in Alina's choice to break up with him. The older woman voiced her concern about Alina's choice of boyfriends, saying her daughter needed a man who had more backbone. She also claimed Ryan would leave her for the first pretty face to cross his path. He never understood why the woman didn't care for him.

I wonder about Anna. . . . Thoughts of seeing the whimsical young woman again nudged him. Alina used to think he feigned interest in her mentally challenged twin. When she learned he genuinely wanted to help and make sweet Anna laugh, Alina cried. Ryan remembered holding her outside of a small café near the Ohio State campus while snow fell in huge flakes and tears streamed down her cheeks.

"I'll love you forever," she'd said.

"And I'll always be here for you—and Anna."

"Oh, Ryan. I want to believe you." She'd sniffed and blinked back the wetness. Her brown eyes had radiated trust and confidence.

"You can." Then he'd lifted her chin and lightly kissed her lips, brushing away the tears with a gloved finger. "If you don't stop crying, icicles are going to grow on your cheeks."

Ryan chased away the memories and tucked all the items back into the part of his heart that he wanted sealed with duct tape. Some memories stay embedded in your heart no matter how hard you try to destroy them.

seven

Thursday, 7:45 a.m.

Ryan poured a fresh cup of coffee and reached for a packet of creamer. Yesterday had been tolerable with Alina. He figured avoiding him emotionally was her way of handling the stress between them. He wondered if a boyfriend played into her personal life, but she had no pictures perched on her desk, and she had never mentioned a man in any of her conversations. He had to admit he'd listened when she took phone calls, and nothing indicated a significant other.

I am as much in love with her now as I was in college.

"There he is, the terminator," a male voice said.

Ryan glanced up to see James leaning against the door of the break room. They were alone, and obviously the foreman saw an opportunity to throw a few bricks. "Since no one else is in here, I gather you're talking to me." He stirred his coffee with a little red plastic stick.

"That's right."

This guy gave him a whole new perspective on the meaning of patience. He tossed the stir stick into a trash can. "Look, James—"

"Mr. Ferguson."

Ryan smiled. "All right, Mr. Ferguson. We got off on the wrong foot."

"We're still there. I mean, you're on the wrong foot. I'm on the side of what is right."

"You're entitled to your opinion." Ryan immediately changed his countenance and threw a gaze aimed to control the situation. "The way I look at it, you have a choice. We can agree you have an attitude problem here and try to work together, or you can head into Fred's office and tell him I fired you. Which will it be?"

"Before or after I crack your face?"

"That's entirely up to you." Ryan leaned against the counter, radiating every bit of confidence he could muster. "I need your knowledge and leadership in this transition, but I don't put up with animosity. Bad attitudes are contagious. I have no qualms about replacing you." He picked up his coffee and made his way past James. "You choose. Let me know soon. I understand there are lots of qualified people looking for work these days."

Fortunately, Ryan's nose stayed intact.

Thursday, 10:30 a.m.

Ryan watched Alina struggle with what he thought was a problem with Neon's software. Why couldn't she simply ask for help? Since Tuesday, he'd sensed her frustration with the accounting reports he requested. Time was money, and he needed the data *she* was supposed to be gathering. The confrontation with James surfaced and left him agitated.

"How are you doing over there?" He hoped he sounded non-threatening. After the break room incident, his private joke about VWMD—verbal weapons of mass destruction—had taken on new emphasis. Undue pressure with the present circumstances could make the following weeks a challenge, to say the least.

"I've done better." Her gaze appeared to be glued to the screen.

"Do you need help?"

She turned in her chair to face him. "Although you explained the technology and the procedure for these reports, I'm having a difficult time assembling the data. I'm sorry."

All business. "No need to apologize. Let me take a look. This can be tricky, especially for one who isn't familiar with our product. Once you have it, the other reports will be a whiz."

She stood from her chair, and he seated himself in front of her computer. One glance told him she'd neglected a final configuration to pull up the necessary data. "Right here, Alina. These codes will get you access to the accounting files."

"Thanks. I thought I'd written down all the steps." She avoided him and made notes on a notepad beside her mouse. "Does this configuration apply to all of Neon's financial records?"

"Yes." Maybe he had bad breath. He reached inside the desk drawer for a peppermint. "Don't hesitate to ask questions. There's no point in wasting time and effort when you need answers."

"I said I thought I had all the instructions before me."

Testy. "And I only suggested you ask the next time."

"I believe I did."

He inwardly counted to ten. Normally, diplomacy ranked high for him, but obviously James and Alina lowered his tolerance level. "Do you need a break? I'd be glad to get you some coffee."

She arose from the side chair and walked across the length of the office. "No thanks. I'm quite capable of getting my own coffee, and I don't need you to patronize me."

He whirled around. "What are you talking about?"

"Right, Ryan. I didn't need access to any code to understand your little condescending remarks about me not working fast enough."

While doing his best to appear emotionless, Ryan tore through his memory bank for the appropriate words to ease her irritation. Where had she come up with such craziness?

"And don't give me a textbook response," she continued. "I simply can't do this. . .this working together."

"You broke up with me, remember? I should be the one feeling uncomfortable, not you."

She gestured around the room. "You're telling me that you have no. . ." She paused. "No uneasiness or doubts about working with me for three months minus one week? That this is purely business and nothing else?"

"I'd be a liar if I said otherwise. I thought we'd talked through this issue the other day."

She crossed her arms over her chest. "It's harder than I thought. I can't think clearly. I can't work. Why didn't you change your brand of cologne?"

He looked startled. "Why didn't *you* change *your* brand of cologne?"

They faced each other. He wanted to go to her, wrap his arms around her, and ask her if there was a way to make things right between them. They could pick up the pieces of their shattered relationship, couldn't they?

"Can't someone else do your job, or someone else complete my part?" The defeat in Alina's voice echoed with desperation.

"And what reason do we give? I've worked with people who hated my guts. We're professionals, not kids fussing over who gets what toy."

"Toys? I appreciate your choice of words. Toys? As in who has a job at the end of three months and who doesn't?"

He wanted to wring her pretty little neck. "Alina, listen to reason."

"I want ground rules." Her voice quivered. What had brought on her emotional onslaught? Had he missed something? *Women—so difficult to read.*

"For what? Is it the lunch and dinner thing? All right. I apologize for asking you to join me." He stood and closed the office door, then turned so no one from the outer office could see or hear the tirade. "What else? I purposely didn't attend your church on Sunday so I wouldn't offend you. I want this settled now, because I have a job to do."

"I'm glad you are so gainfully employed." A crack of thunder rattled the office windows.

"What can I do, Alina, but make recommendations?"

She turned her back on him. "I wouldn't want you to venture outside of your professional ethics."

"Sarcasm won't help the issues between us."

She stiffened. "You don't understand, do you?"

"How can I? You ended the relationship. You refused to talk to me then, and you're acting the same way now. Would you please turn around?"

"Maybe later."

The urge to grab and shake her sped across his mind. Lightning streaked across the sky. Within seconds, thunder split the air again. "Great weather. Goes with our amicable discussion," he said. "You asked for ground rules. What did you have in mind?"

She stood frozen, as though moving might cause her to change her mind. "Do you despise me?"

That's a ground rule for working together? "No. Do you want me to?"

"I'm asking the questions."

He blew out a heavy sigh. "No, I don't despise you. Anything else?"

"It would be beneficial if I knew you had a girlfriend."

"Not at the present. If it makes you feel any better, I'd much prefer you had a boyfriend. Are you seeing anyone?"

"I'm still asking the questions, but for the record I don't have one of those. If you see the transition will be shorter than three months, would you call that to my attention?"

"Certainly. It's not my desire to have you go one day without an income, other than your severance pay."

"The letter of recommendation—will it be affected by our past?"

"Negative again." He could tell she was working her way up to something.

Before another word was spoken, Deidre opened the door. "In case you haven't figured it out, a nasty storm is headed our way. Tornado warnings, too. Want me to order out for lunch?"

"Sure," Ryan said. In one breath he welcomed the interruption, but nothing had been settled between them, simply more of the same. One day he'd corner Alina and get his answers. He'd waited six years; he could endure a little while longer. But what was she about to say?

❧

Friday, 11:30 a.m.

Alina needed to talk to someone, and that someone was Deidre.

Ryan and Fred were in a meeting, and the lunch hour fast approached. She moved from her desk and out of the office to her dear friend. "How about a little walk? I need to sort out some things before I go nuts."

"Sure thing." Deidre set the phone on voice mail and grabbed her coat. Outside, the sky held a tint of gray, more like rain clouds than snow. Yesterday's storm had passed over Radisen with only a mild electrical storm. They walked toward town. Although neither had said a word about the Bake Shoppe a few blocks down, Alina knew they'd end up there.

"Hope those clouds head in the opposite direction. I've had enough rain for a while. The creeks are up," Deidre said.

"Uh-huh. The weather befits my mood, but a heavy dose of sunlight would help me crawl out of this pit."

"So what is making you crazy, girlfriend?"

"In short, working with Ryan makes me behave like a teenager on hormonal overdrive," Alina blurted out.

"Is he obnoxious? Rude?"

Alina shook her head. "Quite the contrary. He's kind, considerate, patient, and understanding."

"Sweetie, I understand this is a debatable point, but are you ready to admit you're still in love with him?"

Did she dare answer that question? "I'm not sure."

"Oh, yes you are."

Alina shrugged. "Yeah, probably so. I wish he'd snap at me or something. I mean, he doesn't let me get by with anything, but I'd feel better if he went completely ballistic."

Deidre laughed, and when Alina considered her last remark, she laughed, too.

They walked a few more steps in silence. "Maybe this walk wasn't such a good idea after all. All I'm doing is dragging you through my problems. I know this business with Flash and Neon isn't all about me, but the relationship thing is definitely all about me and Ryan."

"Let's talk about you two. How did you meet?"

"At college. It was one of those storybook moments in the

library where the only place to sit and study was right beside him." Alina tilted her head. "I remember our first date." At least with the wind hitting her in the face, she didn't have to look at Deidre, only talk. "My wild, crazy mother nearly did us both in."

"Tell me all of it."

Alina smiled. "I brought Ryan home to meet Mom. You know, the approval thing. Anyway, Mom found out we planned to go shopping and invited herself."

Deidre moaned. "From what you've told me about your mother, that had to be. . .well, unusual."

"She had her pleasant moments, and she could be quite charming. This was one of those times, and she wanted to check out this guy dating her daughter."

"That obvious?"

"Oh yeah." Alina laughed. "She wanted to take her car, and Ryan got stuck in the backseat. I noticed she kept staring at him in the rearview mirror. Later he told me he thought he'd grown warts. Anyway, during lunch she made the announcement that she wanted to give Ryan a perm."

"You're kidding. A perm? What did he say?"

"Deidre, he agreed! You should have seen him then. He wore his blond hair to his shoulders. It was thick and gorgeous. He looked more like a California surfer than a native Ohioan."

"Why did he agree to such a ridiculous suggestion?"

"Said he was trying to impress her." Alina laughed again. "Right in the middle of rolling up the perm, she decided one side was a little longer than the other. She got out her scissors, and in the process of trimming his hair, she accidentally clipped his ear. His poor ear bled and bled. Ryan just sat there holding his ear while Mom wound his hair around those perm rods."

They both broke into hysterics. "I'll never forget when she took out all the rods and dried it. She said, 'Look at all those pretty waves.' And kissed him on the cheek."

"How did Ryan react?"

"We had to stop at a drugstore and purchase one of those

hair-straightening kits. Then I had to fix the mess Mom made. He never complained, but we had plenty of laughs about it."

Deidre glanced up at the rolling clouds. "What if he wanted to get back together?"

Alina hesitated. As much as she wanted Ryan in her life. . . "The problems are still there, Deidre. Nothing's changed. They've only grown worse. Festered."

"The bottom line is you're in love with the man, yet you're convinced the relationship will never work out."

"Yes. You've put into one sentence what I can't seem to grasp."

"By whose standards? Yours or his?"

"Mine, but if he knew the truth, his standards would reveal the same thing."

"Sounds complicated."

"It is. And I'm praying about it all. Right now I feel God has played a horrible joke on me. I'm losing sleep, and my work is suffering. All because I have to work with Ryan every day. Three months is forever." Alina glanced at her friend. "Dramatics are not my normal way of handling crises. Does that tell you anything?"

Deidre smiled. "The heart doesn't understand logic and time. What about a stop at our favorite Bake Shoppe?"

"Oh, why not. Lately I either have no appetite or consume everything in sight."

"You really have it bad." When Deidre opened the door of the shop, the tantalizing smells of rich pastries and deli delights wafted around them.

Alina enjoyed the specialties there, but today her heart longed for more than food.

eight

"How are you and Ryan getting along?" Marta asked as she and Alina rode horses across the pasture at Fred and Marta's farm. Green spots showed here and there, with promises of spring, but March could deceive them with another jolt of ice and snow.

"Nothing like being blunt." Alina laughed, but the familiar ache swelled in her heart. "As well as can be expected. I think Ryan is pleased with our progress."

"You've had four full days together, and I don't see any battle scars."

"None visible anyway," Alina said.

The radiant smile, so much a part of Marta, faded, and sympathy took its place. "I'm joking about working with Ryan, and truthfully I have no idea how difficult this must be for you. You're in our prayers, and we will do all we can in your pursuit of another job. When Fred learned your position would be eliminated, he wanted to back out, but between the doctor, the kids, and me, we convinced him his health had to take priority. I hope you understand."

"I do, and I wouldn't have it any other way. Really, I *was* angry when I first got the news about the buyout. Then when I learned the reasons why, I felt horrible for creating such a fuss."

Marta stopped her horse. "I'm going to tell you something, and I don't want a word of it leaked out to the others."

The seriousness in Marta's voice caused Alina to rein her horse in. "Of course. What's wrong?"

"Fred's health is worse than what he's telling people."

"Isn't the medication helping?" Alina asked.

"Yes, but he has to take off about thirty pounds. The stress is too much on his heart." Marta shrugged. "Last week he had a spell, and I believe it fell under the category of a light heart attack. The doctor is talking about a quadruple bypass."

Alina gasped. "Are you sure? Have you obtained another opinion?"

"Oh yes. They want him to have some additional testing and lose the weight before surgery. Naturally, Fred doesn't have the time for such nonsense—as he puts it—until he gets a breather at work."

"That's crazy. He needs to be in the hospital now. We can handle Flash."

Marta patted the mare's neck. "He'd like to think he can't leave the company for the surgery and required recuperation. In any event, if you'd remember him in your prayers, I'd appreciate it."

"You got it. I wonder if any of us could do anything to keep his life a little calmer."

"Whatever you do, it can't look like it came from me, or I'm in trouble."

"I'll run it by you before we act," Alina said. "In the meantime, I'll look for ways to eliminate any undue stress."

Marta shook her head. "Whatever stress you can keep from him is good. I want my Fred to enjoy retirement. He's committed to the weight loss, but unloading work burdens is a whole new problem. That's the real reason I wanted to know about your and Ryan's working relationship. It's a favor, I guess."

Alina took a deep breath, hoping the discussion didn't venture too far into forbidden territory. "Ryan represents a level of professionalism that I need to attain. I have much to learn from him. Some of the others are bitter and blame Neon for pressuring Fred into selling, but I want to give them a good role model. Let's pray God softens their hearts so the burden is less on Fred."

"Even though that's not what happened? He contacted

Neon to see if they were interested in purchasing Flash."

Alina hesitated. She refused to lie, and the truth bordered on more than she cared to confess. "For some of them, that fact doesn't matter. In any event, I'm committed to finishing strong." She forced a chuckle with the cliché. "Fred needs to take it easy, and I'll do all I can. I'm sure this week will be easier. Ryan is not demanding at all, and he could be under the circumstances."

"Fred likes him and says Ryan comes highly recommended from Neon."

"I can see why. I suppose he told you Ryan joined the Tuesday morning Bible study."

"Right, and he came to a Friday night men's study at our church. That's a positive step no matter how you look at it. I have to believe Ryan is praying for things to smooth out." Marta pulled off one of her gloves to allow a drop of rain to fall into her palm. She frowned. "I'm ready for lots of sunshine in more ways than the weather. Say, have you updated your résumé?"

"Sure have. Even made a couple of inquiries, but I need to work on it a little more." Alina wanted the topic to change—to anything but work and Ryan.

The two moved their horses to a ridge overlooking a clump of barren trees where they could see through the limbs. In the distance, the Ohio River, swollen from the thawing snow, flowed lazily. With the sky a tinge of gray, the water reflected the same gloomy tint.

"No matter what the season," Marta said, "I always have to look at the river, study it as though I'm checking the temperament of an old friend. Not sure why, except the river symbolizes that no matter what crisis plagues us, life continues its ebb and flow." She turned to Alina. "Some things were put here to show us the majesty of God's creation."

"I find it hypnotizing."

"I love the river and fear it at the same time, all that tremendous power within the banks of Ohio and Kentucky. No wonder the Native Americans revered it."

Marta's calm reflections soothed Alina's restless spirit. She welcomed the change of pace and the insight.

"Can you imagine paddling a canoe way out there?" Marta asked. "I'd be petrified, and I'm rather daring."

Alina pointed to a barge making its way downstream, most likely with a load of coal. "One of those or a ferry is more my style."

The two laughed and watched the barge inch its way along.

"Alina."

She turned to face the woman of wisdom. "God has a plan, and His purpose will unfold just like the river rises and falls. He will see you through the next few months with blessings far more than you could ever dream. I feel this so deeply that I had to share it."

"I have to believe those very same things," Alina said. "Without His promises, I'd give up." She blinked back a few tears. The urge to tell this wise woman about Ryan nibbled at her heart, but it was best that her secret stay intact. Fred and Marta were concerned about the decision they'd made regarding Flash, and Alina loved them dearly. If they learned the truth, they'd feel even worse.

❧

Monday, 4:00 a.m.

Ryan stared at the clock. The large numbers glared in red. *Why am I awake at four in the morning?* He recalled his mother's words. "If God wakes you in the middle of the night, it's a direct line. Better listen to what He has to say."

Okay, Lord, I'm listening, or am I supposed to be praying for someone? For the next few moments, Ryan prayed for everyone he could think of. Still, sleep evaded him.

Lord, is this about the job offer in Columbus? Am I supposed to take it? Decline? As good as the promotion sounded, he feared jumping into a new position. His parents would love having him around, although they traveled a lot since retiring. He chuckled. All of this could be so he'd keep watch on his parents' home and feed the dog when they were gone. He ought to seek out their advice, or at least run the idea past them. *Never hurts to gather wise counsel.* Ryan switched on the light above his nightstand and reached for the notepad. He jotted down a reminder to call Mom and Dad.

Lord, is this break into my sleep about Alina? Is she having a tougher time than I think with this transition? Of course, the whole buyout had to be overwhelming: losing her job and all the insecurities surrounding a possible career change and relocation. To top it off, she had to work with him. Back in college, she'd exhibited extraordinary strength except when it came to dealing with her mother. Perhaps her mother was ill and Alina needed to take care of her, too. He took a deep breath and weighed the merits of calling her—to check on her. She most likely wouldn't appreciate being wakened, but if something was wrong, he could offer help.

The urge to phone Alina refused to let up. His gaze rested on his cell phone by his computer. Even his toes tingled. Finally he crawled from the bed and looked for her number in his Flash contacts. A part of him figured he was asking for trouble—possibly the harassment suit that often entered his mind. He cringed; a lawsuit would take care of any promotions. Yet. . .what if someone was trying to break into her home, or she'd received devastating news? Ryan ignored the reservations and punched in her number on his cell. She answered on the first ring.

"Alina, this is Ryan. Are you all right?"

"Ryan?" She yawned. "Yes, I'm fine. Why?"

"I had this weird feeling you might need help."

"Not at all. For some reason I woke up and haven't been able to go back to sleep."

He smiled and leaned back on the bed. "Me, too. I—I feel really stupid about this call. And you're fine?"

"Yes, unless you have a cure for insomnia."

"I usually pray."

"Yeah, I remember what your mother used to say."

She hasn't forgotten. "So were you praying for me?"

"Do you fancy yourself at the top of my list?" He loved the teasing in her voice.

"Sorry. A guy can hope." Silence. The wrong thing to say. "Did you have a good weekend?"

"As a matter of fact, I did. I took Anna outside on Saturday afternoon, and we had a picnic of sorts. A little chilly, but I wrapped her up good. Then today, Marta, Fred's wife, and I rode horses on their property. I guess that was yesterday. What about you?"

Lonesome and thinking about the past echoed through his mind, but he shoved it aside. "Saturday I drove into Kentucky and enjoyed a bit of early spring. Sunday I attended a church here in Radisen, grabbed a to-go lunch, jogged a few miles, and read a great novel. Oh, and I took a nap. Old age must be settling in." He hesitated. "Do you know why you woke up so early?"

"Not a clue."

So I could call? "Guess I should let you try to sleep again."

She yawned again. "It's nearly four thirty, and we have to work today."

"See you in a few hours, and thanks for understanding about my early morning call. It's—it's been good talking to you." Ryan disconnected the call and set his cell phone on the nightstand. Wide awake, he headed for his laptop to get a head start on the day. He hoped the rest of the day made more sense than these last few minutes.

≈

Vulnerable best described how Alina felt. She should have exploded at Ryan for calling at such a horrible hour. Instead, she chatted away like the time or their business relationship meant nothing—like a giddy teenager. Why, she nearly flirted with him. How utterly disgusting.

If only she hadn't been awake to begin with—and thinking about him. And yes, she'd been talking to God about the mess in her life, and she'd shed buckets of tears in the process. In a peculiar way, it seemed perfectly logical that Ryan should call a little after four in the morning. After all, he'd occupied her thoughts since before three.

If she didn't watch her every step, Ryan would discover her feelings for him. How would she handle that catastrophe? Alina groaned and punched her pillow. The thought of him learning about the love buried in her heart for over six years sent her stomach into a twist worse than a roller-coaster ride.

Unable to sleep, she threw back the blankets and headed for the shower. With all this extra time, she'd edit her résumé and send it to a few prospective employers. Two companies in Columbus had indicated interest. The commute from Columbus to Anna's home was about an hour and a half. Definitely doable.

She stretched. About two o'clock this afternoon, she'd be searching the drawers in the break room for toothpicks to hold her eyes open. *Thank you very much, Mr. Ryan Erikson. One more time you succeeded in robbing me of precious sleep.* He held the record for the cause of her insomnia. If only. . .the truth could be hidden from him, but she feared he'd one day learn her secret.

A tear slipped from her eye and rolled down her cheek. Emotional rain. Love showers. A flood of regret. No matter how she termed it, remorse always came in the form of Ryan Erikson.

nine

"Alina, how are things with the terminator?" James poked his head inside her office right after Ryan disappeared with Deidre to access records on the second floor.

James's stance on the buyout had nearly gotten the best of her on numerous occasions. "Your attitude is not my idea of cooperation. Neither is it a way to respect Fred. Even if you don't like Ryan, you could still honor Fred's request."

"So he's won you over? I thought you had more sense than to side with the enemy." He stuffed his hands in his jeans pockets. "I'm disappointed in you."

"Ryan is not the enemy, and neither is Neon. Fred went to them when his health dictated retirement and he realized customers needed better service. You know that as well as I do. And you, of all people, should recognize Flash's inability to stay up-to-date with technology."

"People here in Radisen are fine with our service. You have a degree that will help you land another job, even if you're one of the unlucky employees who won't have one. I don't have a college education, and neither do my guys. We have families to feed. Kids to clothe. Rent to pay. You don't have a clue about finances."

Alina's temperature gauge registered above the boiling point, and anger took over. She stood and clenched her fists. "If you don't leave my office this instant, I will go to Fred with the recommendation that he replace you. Then you can tell Becky and the kids how you lost your job." She took a deep breath, and common sense flowed back into her veins. "James, you've been coming to Bible study for the past few months. Your family has regularly attended church. Harboring bitterness and resentment is not what God wants for any of us. I admit I'm having a hard time with the buyout, but I want to please God and do my best for Him. By improving my attitude, I help Fred." She took a deep breath. "I apologize for spewing at you—not for the words but for how I said them."

James's jaw tightened, and he whirled around. The keys on his belt jingled down the hall. Alina stood and watched him head back to where the servicemen gathered when not on calls. He might not have appreciated what she said, but she felt God had spoken to James through her words. Ironic, yet so like her heavenly Father.

"Good job," Deidre said.

Alina turned to see her friend grinning like a child with a bag of candy. "You heard?"

"Every word. James received a heavy dose of reality from you. He's been stirring up trouble among the employees, and I don't like it. Sooner or later he'll have to make a choice, or Fred and Ryan will have him escorted out the door."

Alina nodded. She swallowed a lump the size of a golf ball. Tears for James Ferguson? Why not? God wept oceans for His children.

"Here comes Ryan now," Deidre said. "I opt for not telling him about your recent visitor."

"He won't hear it from my lips."

"Have either of you seen James?" Ryan asked a moment later. "We have an appointment."

"I saw him head that way," Alina said, pointing toward the back. "He's probably with the servicemen."

"Thanks. We're supposed to go on a few calls together."

"With James?" Deidre's face paled.

"Yeah. If I don't return, call out the National Guard." Ryan chuckled, but Alina didn't think it was a bit funny.

"Who else is going?" Alina asked. "Just in case we get worried." She forced a smile.

"No one. Oh, he's harmless. All talk. See you later." Ryan

strolled down the same hall that James had taken.

Alina crossed her arms over her chest. "Remind me never to take a job like Ryan's."

"Certainly not without disability insurance."

"Oh, you are witty." She shrugged. "I hope James doesn't lose his temper."

"Be careful. Your heart is showing." Deidre wagged a finger at her.

"I'm going on Fred's recommendation. Fred likes him, and I like Fred."

"Hey, girlfriend, this is Deidre here. Don't forget, I know the bottom line."

≈

Thursday, 10:15 a.m.

Ryan realized he'd stepped into dangerous territory when he agreed to ride with James on the afternoon calls. From his past dealings with employees who openly displayed hostility, Ryan believed James's problem was gut-wrenching fear. Some men clothed themselves with a macho image in times of distress instead of seeking out answers to the problems that affected their ego.

When he first read James's file and saw his qualifications and his outstanding record, Ryan wanted to keep him on board. But the man's belligerent attitude had to change, or James would be gone by Monday morning. Threats and accusations might work in the pool hall, but not in the business world where upper management called the shots.

James stood outside his van with a couple of other servicemen. From the venom-tipped darts the man's eyes aimed at Ryan, he gathered the afternoon would be either incredibly long or incredibly short. James still hadn't given him an answer about whether he planned to use his skills and leadership abilities or hit the road. Ryan should have forced his hand the day James cornered him in the break room. Instead he let it ride, and nothing had been resolved. Not good in the management department.

Ryan greeted the other men, then turned to James without waiting for a response. "I'm ready if you are."

James failed to reply but moved toward the driver's side of the van. "You men have work to do. Get at it." He laughed and waved.

Once inside the van, Ryan took out a clipboard.

"Am I being tested?"

He managed a laugh for James's benefit. "I already know your abilities. This is for me to evaluate any differences between the ways Flash and Neon personnel handle service calls. You may have a procedure that we need to incorporate or the other way around."

"I'm not rude to customers, if that's what you're wondering."

Nice added touch. "Fred respects the work you do. If customers complained, he wouldn't have kept you working for the past five years."

"So it *is* a test." *Caustic* best described James's tone.

Ryan ignored him. No point in fueling an argument. They bumped down the street, hitting every pothole. He refused to complain. Framed children's photos attached to pieces of leather swung back and forth from the rearview mirror.

"Those are your children?" Ryan asked.

"Yeah. Have four of them."

"How old are they?"

"Jonathon's eight, Jarrod's seven, Jenna's five, and Jason's three."

Ryan hadn't asked for names. Maybe he could get inside James's heart through his kids, and they were a good-looking bunch. The older boy posed with a ball. "So the oldest plays soccer?"

"And Jenna, although Jarrod is more interested in baseball and piano."

"That's a different combination." *What a breakthrough. He's talking to me.*

"My wife wants them to be exposed to everything. Whatever

they're good at will help when it comes around to college scholarship time."

So James cared about his family. They weren't rug rats or liabilities, but his children. "And education is expensive," Ryan said. "I had a few grants, but mostly I worked my way through."

"I took you for the family-money kind of guy."

Ryan shook his head. "Nope, my parents were blue-collar workers who instilled in us the value of learning."

"Are you saying something's wrong with blue-collar people?"

Great, here it comes: animosity barreling down the field. "Not at all. I'm proud of my folks. They helped me see the value of hard work."

The van pulled to a stop in front of a home. "Look, I'm not into small talk or swapping family stories, especially with someone I don't like. But I have a job to do and a family to support."

"I understand."

"I doubt it. What I'm saying is you wanted my cooperation, and I'll give it."

"Thank you."

"No need. This is for Fred. He gave me a job and trained me when no one else was interested."

"I'll be blunt here. You have the know-how to keep the service department running smoothly. I'd like to recommend Neon keep you on as foreman of the crew, but I have to see for myself that you're willing to cooperate with the ones running the show."

"Fair enough, but I don't have to like you."

"I'm not asking for flowers and candy, just respect and a good day's work."

"I'll see what I can do."

Ryan felt like he'd made a little headway. "And for the record, Neon pays for employees who want to continue their education as long as it will benefit their current job. They also give out thousands of dollars in college scholarships to employees' kids."

James opened his door. "Is all that in a handbook somewhere?"

"Yes, and also online."

"I don't have computer skills, and I hear Neon keeps all of their service calls there. Maybe I could take a class on that." James peered at him. "Don't be blowing smoke about any of this. You might have some of the other folks on your side, but I'm not easily convinced."

"Trust takes time."

"So does raising kids."

&

Thursday, 8:30 p.m.

Alina switched off the vacuum, unplugged it, and wound the cord around the handle. Housecleaning done for another week. She snatched up the furniture polish and tucked it under her arm along with the dust cloth as she pushed the vacuum to the closet. *My whole apartment smells yummy-lemon and sparkles with a dust-free sheen.* She smiled. *Maybe I should consider going into television and doing commercials.*

She glanced around at the eclectic collection of antiques and sleek contemporary designs mixed with vibrant reds and bright yellows. A room to fit her every mood. Most of the time, she grappled with which mood fit her that day.

At the moment her stomach growled for food. Some days she overloaded on coffee, chocolate, and peanut butter and pickle sandwiches, and other days she ate like a Victorian lady with dainty amounts of healthful, no-nonsense food. At this very moment, a can of tomato soup with sprinkles of basil and a heavy dose of garlic croutons sounded very appetizing.

After washing her hands, she reached for the can of soup and the opener from a drawer that was in dire need of organization. Tomorrow night she'd tackle the clutter. Right now, she simply wanted to relax.

How exciting. She planned to clean drawers on a Friday night. Unfortunately, her life had been like this for the past six years. No hope for a man to fill her dreams; she had responsibilities a man would never understand.

Alina took a deep breath and flipped on the radio. She refused to start in with the woe-is-me list. A knock at the door surprised her. She made her way to the door and took a glimpse through the peephole, then flung it open.

"Hi, Deidre. Come on in. What brings you in from the farm?"

She laughed and held up a plastic-covered dish. "This is Thursday, cleaning night, and you normally don't eat until about now."

"Vietnamese food?" Alina lifted the lid. The aroma of vegetables was intoxicating. "Oh, this is heavenly."

"It's still warm, so grab a fork. I have a few minutes before Clay goes nuts getting the kids bathed and ready for bed. He's been on the tractor all day."

Alina grinned. "And to think I was about to open a can of soup."

"Well, I have another reason for being here. I wanted to see the English washstand you just bought."

"It's in my bathroom. Take a look and I'll get you a glass of iced tea." She pulled out a couple of glasses and opened the fridge.

"It's beautiful," Deidre called. "And it fits in here nicely."

"Thanks. I got it for a good price."

Deidre reappeared in the kitchen. She tilted her head. Confusion etched lines in her face. "Alina, I have a question."

"Sure, fire away—and no, you can't have my washstand."

"Maybe this is none of my business."

Deidre's concern nudged Alina's conscience. "Go ahead. Bringing me Vietnamese food entitles you to ask anything."

"Has Ryan's picture always been on your dresser?"

Alina startled. Why hadn't she remembered to put the picture of them away? "Ah. . .no. I found it in my closet the other day and forgot to put it back."

"Let's sit down and talk." Deidre pointed to the sofa. "This is your girlfriend here, and besides bringing you dinner, I want to have a heart-to-heart talk about your problem with Ryan."

With anyone else Alina would have danced around the

situation and laughed off any implications of her feelings for Ryan. But this was Deidre. "All right, but can I eat while we talk?"

Deidre eased into an antique rocker. "Sure, but don't use your fingers. It's not polite, and I don't want you fainting from lack of food." Her shoulders lifted and fell. "Seriously, have you noticed the way Ryan looks at you?"

Alina's eyes widened. "Are you serious?"

"Sometimes I twist around in my chair to see what's happening in your office. At first it was to make sure you two weren't killing each other, but now it's to see how many times I can find Ryan staring at your back."

Alina sat on the edge of her sofa. "He's probably concentrating on something."

"My point exactly."

Alina waved her fork. "You're seeing things. Besides, I'm very careful to make sure he doesn't get the wrong impression. Oh, this is good." Her heart thumped against her chest. Was Deidre right?

"Alina, what happens when the others notice, too?"

"That bad? I mean, I don't want to be rude." Alina leaned back on the sofa. She couldn't hide the turmoil any longer. "What am I to do? Are you sure he's staring at me?"

"There's a look a man gives a woman when they are working together professionally. There's also a look of admiration a man gives a woman from time to time. There's also a look a man can give that deserves a slap. Then there's the look of a man in love—and he can't disguise it. Ryan is as much in love with you as you are with him."

"Since when did you become an expert on love?"

"I was born a woman."

The impact of Deidre's words gave Alina's stomach a funny little flip. "No matter what you think you saw, nothing can come of it."

"Why? Did he betray you in college and now you can't forgive him or trust him?"

Alina set the food on the coffee table in front of her. "He never gave me a reason not to trust him. It's Anna. I can't ask a man to share me with my mentally challenged sister. She's my responsibility. What if I married and my husband wanted children? I couldn't get pregnant, because then I'd have to quit my job or take a leave of absence. Who would pay for Anna's care?"

Deidre stood and walked across the room. When she faced Alina again, her eyes moistened. "You're denying yourself and any potential husband happiness because of money? Alina, aren't you doubting God in this? If you trust Him with your soul, why not trust Him to provide for Anna?"

A wave of sickness swept over her. She swallowed hard. "Believe me, this problem is complicated, and parts of it are real. . .ugly. Walking away from love is my lot in life. Once this transition is completed, Ryan will be gone and I'll be able to deal with life again."

"But you love a good, Christian man, and I believe he loves you. Would you simply pray about the situation? Ask God what He wants for your life?"

Alina nodded. If she verbally agreed to Deidre's request, she'd get blubbery and embarrass herself. "I have. Many times. But I promise you, I'll go to Him again."

Deidre sat down by Alina and took her hand. "Don't you find it more than a quirk of circumstance that he is at Flash, working alongside you? I don't know about you, but I don't believe in coincidence or luck. This is at the hand of God, and for some reason I can't help believing it's for you two to be together."

Alina couldn't tell her friend the truth. The harsh reality of Alina's and Anna's lives lay embedded in a secret place no one could enter. Even God didn't look at such darkness.

ten

Alina crumpled her pillow and stared up at the ceiling. Another sleepless night. When would this end? Mid-June, when Ryan left Flash and returned to California? She worked with him all day, then thought about him all night. During the day, her stomach did funny little flips that left her physically ill, and at night she had heartburn. If love did this to a person, she was in line for a cruel death.

But she hadn't gone through any of this nonsense in college. She'd been deliriously happy. Every moment with Ryan filled her with excitement and longing for the next and the next. *Better to have loved and lost than never to have loved at all.* She'd heard that line all of her life and never did believe it.

Finally Alina decided to brew a cup of decaf herbal tea in the hope of coaxing her body to sleep. Once she squeezed the tea bag and lifted the cup to her lips, it occurred to her that between cleaning her apartment and then Deidre's visit, she hadn't checked her e-mail yet. Seated at her desk with mouse in hand, she clicked on SEND AND RECEIVE. She blinked at the spam and hit the DELETE key. A message popped up from Ryan's Neon account. Why would he e-mail her rather than pick up the phone or wait until the morning? She clicked on the message.

Alina,
  I can picture you asking yourself why I'm sending you a message when I'll see you in the morning. Despite the fact I'd like to project the image of a suave man of the world—confident, intellectual, business savvy, on the next cover of a

*business magazine, etc. (don't laugh)—the kid in me fumbles
when it comes to you. Seems like I say or do the wrong thing
on an ongoing basis. My goal is to put our past behind us and
for us to go forward as two intelligent professional people who
have a job to do. In the beginning, when the transition work
began, I thought I could handle our relationship just fine. And
I really can, but sometimes I lack proper business etiquette. My
point is, when I don't explain a procedure correctly or if I come
across as irritated about a question, please forgive me. The
problem is most likely mine.*

    Have a good evening. Tomorrow's Friday!

Ryan

She reached to delete the message but stopped. A longing
to hold on to whatever she could with Ryan kept her from
sending the message into the trash can on her computer. Like
keeping the photograph of them in their college days, holding
on to a few treasured words seemed innocent enough. She
clicked REPLY and stared at the screen. . .what to say. . .what
not to say.

Ryan,
    *No problem. We as humans have emotions that can
be hard to manage. I hope we can finish this project for
the good of Neon and Flash without letting our personal
lives get in the picture. I appreciate your goal of utmost
professionalism.*

Alina

She reread the reply several times to make sure it didn't
sound in the least encouraging. Another thought ran through
her mind, and she added a line.

    *Do not hesitate to point out my errors or behavior that you
find incompatible with a sound working relationship. This is
important to me.*

Cold as a fish was the perfect cliché to describe her response. The distance between them had to widen, or she'd never make it for three months. She'd do anything to guard her defenses. Ryan must never discover the truth.

Tomorrow, she vowed—no, tomorrow *with* God's help— she'd do a better job at behaving like a godly woman. Her e-mail response to Ryan paved the way for a new and improved Alina. Tonight she'd make a list of priorities in seeking new employment. She needed to send out tons of résumés, not just a few. Every name and address that called for her qualifications was a potential employer.

While online, she searched through the various postings from firms who were looking for qualified personnel. Unfortunately, until this very minute her mind had been too scattered to do anything but search out a few Web sites. When Alina realized her frazzled brain wasn't retaining a thing about the job market, she powered down the computer and flipped on the TV. A program about people makeovers grabbed her attention. A very homely young woman and an equally unattractive man pled their cases, telling how physical changes in their bodies would make them happy. Granted, the two looked great after the weeks of intense physical changes. Friends and family cried, and so did Alina. But what about the rest of those who were miserable when life didn't go their way? All the tummy tucks, nose jobs, liposuction, new clothes, hairdos, and expensive makeup in the world wouldn't soothe the regrets scarring her heart. And if she elected to have all those things done to her body, who'd care?

What about emotional makeovers? Or better yet, spiritual makeovers? How about a makeover guaranteed to get an old love off your mind? Liposuction of the heart would do it.

≈

Friday, 5:45 a.m.

Alina awoke to the sound of rain pelting the roof. Storms had raged all night with ear-piercing thunder and flashes of lightning that lit up the sky in one jagged pattern after another. Sirens blared with the storm's fury, no doubt en route to fires caused by the lightning. She always said a quick prayer for those who were affected tragically by electrical storms—the fear of which she'd never completely overcome. Alina snuggled under fresh, clean-smelling linens until the thunder faded to rumblings in the distance. The thought of nature pitching a curve when she wanted to enjoy birds singing their accolades to spring had just enough leverage to shove her into a foul mood.

Even if nature had accommodated her sleeping hours, rest still would have evaded her. Images from the past and worries about the future plagued her thoughts. Deidre's visit and Ryan's e-mail did little to soothe the turmoil inside her. Ryan had correctly assessed the situation between them a few days ago: *"Great weather. Goes with our amicable discussion."*

Pushing away the nightmares that had stalked her for over twenty-five years, she forced herself upright. The idea of staying at home and curling up with a good book sounded cozy. She loved her little home with its eclectic mixture of antiques and sleek modern designs, and little there hinted of job loss or Ryan Erikson, except the telltale photograph. *Dream on, Alina.* Flash Communications and her responsibilities called her from the warm, comfortable bed to the shower, to work. Self-pity time was over. Reality edged in like the gray dawn. In fact, she'd head in early and get a good start on the day's work.

At least the storm had passed. She had a phobia about standing in the midst of running water during an electrical storm, and this morning she craved gallons of hot water to soothe her tired body. With the coffee set to brew, Alina tuned in the radio only to hear the weather forecaster predict more rain to come.

"Going to need your umbrellas today," the forecaster said, with too much perkiness. "Winds will be gusty and out of the north. Rain mixed with thunderstorms will be with us today as well as through the weekend. By Sunday night, freezing temperatures will change the rain to snow."

"You are making my day," Alina said. "I want sunshine," she said as she slipped in a CD to play, "and jazz."

Yesterday's mail caught her attention. She'd stacked it last night before her cleaning spurt without taking the time to open it. She spied a letter from Homeward Hills nestled among a heap of solicitations, as well as a final credit card bill. Hallelujah, she'd met her goal of paying it off. Now the card was officially in her drawer for emergency use only. Alina picked up the envelope from Anna's home and slipped her fingers under the flap to open it. A personal letter spoke of the home's outstanding credentials, complete with glowing testimonials from those who had families housed there, hers included. Near the bottom, an item jumped up with such intensity that she repeated it aloud.

"Due to our commitment of providing excellent care to all of our residents and meeting the rising costs of our high standards, we find it necessary to raise the rates at Homeward Hills 10 percent, effective May 1. We have not had a price increase in our services during the past four years, and we believe the modest amount will help ensure our quality performance for your loved ones."

She moaned. "My life is a joke." Determined not to give in to depression, Alina folded the letter and placed it back inside the envelope. Today she'd take on the role of Scarlett O'Hara and think about how she'd pay for Anna's care another day. No point in wasting brain cells about a matter she couldn't do a thing about.

In less than an hour, Alina emptied the pot of strong coffee, drank a bottle of water, gulped down a fistful of vitamins with orange juice, and ran for her car just as the rain turned into a downpour. Donuts sounded good—a sugar high to go along with all the caffeine. She ate too much of the grease and sugar variety, but some days donuts called her name, and she couldn't say no.

With the rhythmic sound of the windshield wipers swiping at the rain falling faster than the little arms could whisk it away, Alina strained to see clearly. Whatever happened to healing rain? The assault reminded her of life's problems: Everything wanted to cloud her vision of the future. With a sigh, she realized her thoughts did not honor God. The future belonged to Him, just as her doubts, her joys, her sorrows, and this incredible love for Ryan.

Once she arrived at Flash and sloshed through the water to the back door, she set her umbrella aside and removed her boots. James and Fred talked near the service room. Alina waved to them. "Good morning. This rain is really nasty—bone-chilling, too."

"Along with life," James said. As usual, he didn't look a bit happy.

She thought to give him another lecture on his crumbling attitude, but the weary look on his face bridled her tongue. "What's wrong?"

Fred cleared his throat. *Must be serious.* "James got some bad news about his little girl."

"Jenna? Is she sick?"

James pulled out his handkerchief and blew his nose. Had the man been crying? Immediately she regretted what she'd been thinking about him.

"Becky took her to the doctor yesterday. Jenna's been complaining of headaches. The doctor ordered testing and X-rays. Looks like she has a brain tumor."

"Oh, James, I'm so sorry. What's the next step?"

"Well, Becky and I are takin' her to the children's hospital in Columbus next Tuesday. We'll see what the doctor says then. I imagine it will need to be removed."

"I told James we'd all be praying for them—a miracle is in order," Fred said.

"Of course." Alina's thoughts scrambled for something she could say to help. "How is Becky holding up?"

"Better than me, I think. I don't want to think of that tumor being a cancer." He shook his head. "We should have taken her to the doctor the first time she complained. Maybe something could have been done."

"How could you have known?" Alina asked. "Do you mind if I call Becky?"

"I'm sure she'd like to hear from you." He turned to Fred. "Thanks for praying with me. Guess this is a real test to see if I believe in all you've said about God." James made his way to the service room, where he would gather up the work orders for the day.

"And I thought I had troubles." Fred watched James disappear. "Reminds me I'm pretty blessed when I learn about another situation far worse than mine. Makes me feel ashamed for wasting time worrying about things that don't really matter."

"I understand exactly what you mean," Alina said. "James is devoted to Becky and those kids. He loves his family like no man I've ever seen. He's a bit rough around the edges, but he's a good husband and father."

"Coping with learning his child had a brain tumor would be a stretch for a man with seasoned faith; I'm hoping this thing doesn't turn James against God." He blew out a heavy sigh. "Jenna's got to come through this, Alina. I'm going to call our pastor. James and Becky definitely need the hand of God through this."

Alina's gaze trailed to the service room. "Sure makes me feel selfish about all my whining. I'll let the staff know about it, if that's all right."

Fred nodded.

eleven

Ryan stepped out of his SUV rental into a puddle of water. A gust of wind snapped his umbrella inside out and sent a torrent of rain straight into him. The huge splash made him feel as though a bucket of cold water had been thrown into his face. If he'd had any doubts before now, he was definitely awake. He raced toward the building, soaking his shoes and much preferring a blizzard. Building snowmen, sledding, and having snowball fights were much more fun than avoiding water. His part of California didn't have weather like this. The idea of facing this again and again—and he would if he accepted the promotion to Neon's VP position in Columbus—took a heavy dose of consideration. He'd moved to the West Coast for milder weather and never missed Ohio's winters. God would have to send a banner across the sky to convince him to move back to old home territory. With a heavy sigh, he realized if it didn't stop raining, he'd be wading to his car after work.

"Did you order this?" he asked Alina once he made it to her office.

"Not exactly, but if this delightful weather dampens your spirit about the transition, you can always come over to the other side. We take recruits here." Alina lifted her head from the computer. She smiled, and her nut-brown eyes sparkled—a rather nice addition to the gloomy morning.

"Very funny. If I didn't know better, I'd say you orchestrated this downpour."

She laughed. "It's amazing what a minor in computer science can do. I learned to manipulate everything with the click of a mouse."

"As in a hacker? But you majored in accounting."

"Oh, that's right. Guess I forgot."

Whatever had grabbed hold of Alina, he hoped it would stay firmly attached. "You're in a good mood."

"Must have been all the sleep I had last night," she said. He raised a brow, and she laughed again. "From our early morning conversation, I guess neither of us slept well."

"Nope. Kept wondering if I should have leased an ark instead of an SUV."

He saw her hesitation and wondered what else would fly out of her mouth.

"Ryan, I'm sorry. I really will try harder to make our working relationship a little smoother."

"And I'll try harder to be more sensitive. I read your reply to my e-mail." He groped for words. "By the way, your sweater looks great." Purple had always done special things to her eyes.

"Thanks." She smiled again. "Hey, do you still like chocolate cream-filled donuts?"

"Do I ever."

She handed him a small white bag. "Here are two and six donut holes as a bonus."

"You remembered my obsession with donut holes. I'm at your mercy for the rest of the day." Thrilled as a little boy with a kite on a windy day, he peeked inside and inhaled the tantalizing aroma. "You fought the rain for this?"

"Yeah." Alina shrugged. "I figured I needed to make a little sacrifice to go along with the apology. It probably won't happen again, so cherish those delicacies."

"How about I head for the break room and get us a couple of coffees? Did you get something for yourself?"

She pointed to another bag. "Sure did."

"Maple cream filling?"

She nodded. "Thanks for the coffee refill. I'm in dire need of more coffee this morning."

"I'm on my way."

"I'll see if I can hack back into the weather and end this

downpour." She paused and tilted her head. "Oh, when you get back, I have something to tell you about James. Not good at all."

He made his way to the door. The man probably was proficient in car bombs, or he'd filed some lawsuit against Ryan. He immediately scolded his thoughts. Totally uncalled for. God loved all His children equally, no favorites.

Alina was in a good mood this morning. For a few moments, he had his Alina back, the girl he met and fell in love with in college. The woman he still loved.

Ryan wanted to jump into a lengthy dialogue with her about all those things he remembered about their college days, but he stopped himself before rehearsing any more questions. The tone of her e-mail left no doubt of her intentions. Strictly business. He'd expected her to not even acknowledge him this morning. Then she brought his favorite donuts. He'd never understand women—never.

But this morning was a step in the right direction, and he refused to ruin it. Alina's emotions were as fragile as one of the Styrofoam cups stacked on the counter beside the coffee machine. Fill it with hot coffee, and it might burn his hands.

In the middle of his reverie, Fred rounded the corner and nearly collided with him. "Oops, almost nailed you there."

Ryan grinned. Even wearing coffee stains on his favorite black knit sweater wouldn't spoil his day. *Hmm, Alina used to compliment me when I wore black.* "Is our meeting on at nine thirty?"

Fred rubbed his jaw. "This weather has brought in a flood of service calls. We might get interrupted."

"No problem. I'd like to observe how you handle service call overload." Ryan moved away from the doorway before someone else surprised him. "When is the storm supposed to end?"

"Weatherman said we're in for rain and more rain." Fred reached for the coffee carafe.

"Does it flood here?"

"Not for years. The Ohio River knows we frown on it overflowing its banks. Except the parking lot, and I think it's lower than the two blocks to downtown."

"If this keeps up, might have to post the river a reminder."

Fred nodded. "We'll see if the temperatures plummet. Then we can all ice-skate around town." Concern swept across his face. "Oh, by the way, James got some bad news last night."

"Alina said she needed to tell me about James. What's the problem?" Guilt took a huge bite out of Ryan's conscience.

"He and his wife learned their little girl has a brain tumor. He's pretty shook up."

He recalled the kids' pictures in James's van, and the sound of his voice when he spoke about them. "I'm sorry. Is he here today?"

"Yeah. Come Tuesday, they're taking the little girl to Columbus Children's Hospital."

Bible study day. "I'll remember them in my prayers."

"I appreciate it; so does he, even if he can't vocalize it. A miracle is in order."

"Thanks for telling me."

Ryan walked to Alina's office with a cup of coffee in each hand. She appeared engrossed in her work, but a faint smile came easily. "Just heard about James's daughter," he said. "Is that what you were planning to tell me?"

She nodded. "Sad, isn't it? Jenna's a precious little girl, and her mother is a very sweet lady. I pray for the doctor's wisdom and peace for James and Becky."

"Fred suggested a miracle." He paused. "You have good insurance here. At least he doesn't have to worry about covering medical costs."

She glanced up at him. Doubt crested her eyes.

"I know what you're thinking. Will James have his job at the end of three months?" He hesitated and lowered his voice. "I'm hoping he and I can come to a working understanding, because he's highly qualified and definitely an asset for Neon." An angry shadow flickered in her eyes. He should have chosen his words more carefully.

"What about Neon's medical insurance?" she asked after a moment passed.

"Our plan is excellent and covers preexisting conditions. His little girl would not suffer for good medical care."

She took a sip of coffee. "I may have to reevaluate my opinion of Neon, even if they don't want my expertise." She wrinkled her nose at him and turned back to her computer.

"Alina, the decision to eliminate your position had nothing to do with your qualifications."

She flashed a smile. "I've come to terms with my termination of employment. Don't give it another thought. I plan to land a job with a 20 percent increase in pay; then I can thank Neon."

But still he wondered.

A crack of thunder caused her to jump. "I absolutely hate electrical storms. That business has to go, along with the deluge beating against the window."

He moved her coffee cup back from the keyboard. She'd nearly knocked it over. The maple-filled donut rested atop a napkin with lipstick smudges on a ragged end. He got a whiff of the maple filling. "Fred assured me this area doesn't flood. I'm taking his word for it, although I soaked my shoes crossing your parking lot."

"It's always been a water trap. To set the record straight, I've been in Radisen over five years, and I've never worried about high water. The buzz around here is if you can get out of the parking lot, you can get anywhere." She couldn't even see out the window through the sheets of water crashing against it. "I imagine it will slow down soon."

Ryan sat at the small desk he'd claimed, with his laptop, coffee, and file folders from yesterday. Time to get a few things done before meeting with Fred. A streak of lightning bolted across the sky, followed by another crack of thunder that shook the windows. *Must have hit something.* He glanced around, certain they'd lose power any minute. *Good thing I have a spare battery and the home office receives backups of all I do.*

The phone rang, and since Deidre had stepped away from her desk, he snatched it up.

"Is Alina available?" a deep male voice said.

"Yes, she is. May I ask who's calling?"

"Frank—her boyfriend." The man chuckled. "You must be new."

Boyfriend? New? The green monster coursed through Ryan's veins faster than the rain filling the ditches. He glanced her way.

"Is it for me?" Alina asked. When he nodded, she picked up the phone on her desk.

"Hey, gorgeous," Frank said. "Are we still on for dinner Saturday night?"

Ryan replaced the phone and listened carefully to Alina's side of the conversation.

"I've missed you, too, and thanks for the roses... How sweet... Yes, I'll be ready... Oh, I don't care where we go... Love you bunches. Bye."

Every nerve in Ryan's body stiffened. Who was this Frank character? And what right did he have sending Alina roses and taking her to dinner? She'd said she didn't have a boyfriend. *"Love you bunches."* Ryan clenched his mouse.

Alina hummed a popular tune from a recent movie, one of those chick flicks in which the couple lived happily ever after. He'd seen it by himself out of boredom. Ryan fumed. At least he'd gotten donuts this morning. All Frank got was a promise for dinner. Maybe Ryan could convince Alina to go to dinner with him tonight. She'd refused him before, but he'd once known how to move her to his way of thinking. Gummy bears used to do the trick. Once he'd turned cartwheels across the front lawn of her dorm while a few buddies serenaded her on guitars.

Suddenly the absurdity of his contemplations hit him square in the face. He was jealous of a man he'd never met and scheming about how to win Alina's affections. His maturity level had dropped to the sixteen-year-old level. *I need a hobby—anything to shove Alina from my mind.*

"If you aren't going to eat your other donut, I will," she said. "I'm starved this morning, and yours has lots of gooey chocolate."

Ryan picked it up and took a generous bite. "Absolutely not. These are the best donuts I've had in years." He broke the rest of it in half. "Okay, I'll make the ultimate sacrifice and split this one and the donut holes."

"You're such a good man."

"Glad you're convinced. If you're going to join my fan club, spread the word. I could use a morale booster."

※

Friday, 10:00 a.m.

Alina had spent many a time wrestling with the reasons she committed to one type of behavior and then proceeded with another. This morning was one of those times. She'd been determined to steer away from Ryan's charms; then she took one look at him, and her senses turned to mush.

Now, as she worked through the reports he needed, he paced the office like a caged cat and seemed to have difficulty concentrating on work. The rain, perhaps? Whatever the reason, he was driving her crazy with his inability to tend to the task. She remembered college days when he fretted over a test. He'd pace and study, usually with a book in his hand. Made her crazy then, too.

"Is the rain bothering you?"

He rattled papers on the workstation between them and walked to the window. "Uh, not really, except it puts me in the mood to take a nap."

"Can I help you find something?"

"No thanks. It's here in one of these stacks."

Neon should have instructed him on how to overcome his inability to organize.

"What are you missing?"

"The stats from yesterday. I need it for a meeting with Fred—a meeting that has already been postponed once due to the weather. I don't want to reschedule again because I can't find this information."

She whirled her chair around and picked up the paper from the corner of the table. Ryan must be tired and trying to compensate by overdosing on sugar and caffeine. Understandable. "Are we getting things done fast enough for Neon?"

"We're right on target. We have three phases to complete, and the accounting portion is the first. The other two phases will be less intense."

She noted his black sweater. With his blond hair and blue eyes, he looked exceptional, but she had no business admiring his clothes or him. "This rain makes me sleepy, too. Hope it lets up by tomorrow."

"Got plans?"

"I spend every Saturday with Anna, and anything else I have going on is easier without all the rain."

"At the rate it's coming down, we might be able to go fly-fishing from the parking lot."

She laughed. "I don't have any bait." She paused. "Are you sure you're not upset?"

"I'm fine." He avoided her gaze as he spoke. "Were you able to download the updates to your virus protection software?"

"Done. And now I'm ready to install Neon's latest software." She wished he wouldn't flash his million-dollar smile. It always knocked her off balance.

"There's access to the program online," he said. "Here, I'll bring it up for you." As he leaned over her chair, his intoxicating cologne filled her senses, her nerve cells, her over-stimulated brain—right down to her toes. "Don't be nervous," he said. "This is easy to install. Once I'm into Neon's network, I'll show you how to access things for the future."

Why did he have all the characteristics she craved in a potential husband? Aside from his good looks, he exuded charm and compassion, and most of all—the one item that mattered to her the most—he loved the Lord.

Three months was a long time to fend off affection.

twelve

Friday, 12:30 p.m.

With the inclement weather clawing at the two-story brick building of Flash Communications, the service department ran one call after another to keep up with the power outages and the normal glitches of maintaining a cable company. Lightning managed to do its share of damage, and customers were demanding immediate repairs. Twice Fred postponed the meeting until they decided to have a working lunch. A delivery boy from the deli nearby battled the downpour and brought soup and sandwiches.

Ryan stood outside Fred's door. The older man gestured with his hands while he talked on the phone. His reddened face indicated trouble. "Do what you can, James," Fred said. "Have dispatch radio the other crews and let them know what the situation is." He motioned for Ryan to come on in and pointed to the food. Ryan smelled what he believed was chicken noodle soup. Comfort food.

"Go ahead and eat," Fred mouthed. Lines creased his forehead. "We'll need to call in a few servicemen for Saturday to get caught up." Fred nodded. "Keep me posted." He hung up the phone and reached for his lunch with both hands. "If it doesn't stop raining soon, we're going to have some big problems."

"Service guys having a hard time?"

"Everything is in slow motion today, plus two of the men called in with the flu. The big problem teeters on whether the low-lying areas flood." Concern rang through the older man's voice. "I have the radio on for weather updates, but every time the phone rings, I turn it down. Have you been listening?"

"Fred, I don't think the rain is supposed to let up before sometime tomorrow."

Fred took a bite of his sub sandwich. He chewed on it while staring out the window. The rain had not slowed, making it difficult to gauge how much had fallen. "Once we're finished eating, I need to meet James. He said one of the servicemen botched up a job yesterday, and the customer wants his cable installation fixed immediately or he'll refuse to pay. I'd like to stop by and see what I can do to smooth things over." He glanced up. "But that is my problem, and it may take awhile to resolve. Do you mind if we shelve our discussion until Monday?"

"No problem. I'd like to tag along while you check on the situation," Ryan said.

"I'd welcome the company. I also want to take a drive down toward the river, just to be assured we aren't in for real trouble with the rain—not just for Flash but for the whole town."

"When was the last flood?"

"About thirty years ago, and a lot of construction has gone on since then. Although builders are aware of a potential problem, concrete can't absorb water. So where's it supposed to drain?" He lifted the lid of his soup. "Good old chicken noodle soup. My dear departed mama made hers from scratch just like this. And she always made a huge pot when it rained."

Thirty minutes later, the two men climbed into a service truck and headed southeast through town. Windshield wipers flew fast and furious. Water spilled over the ditches, but none flowed into the streets.

"A little more and the water will flood the streets," Fred said. "And this is not a low spot. If this rain would quit, the drains could handle the overflow. As it is, there's no place for any of it." Fred glanced over at Ryan. "Don't mind me. I'm just an old man complaining about the weather. My knees ache, and I'm mad about the lousy job the serviceman did yesterday."

"I'd complain, too." Ryan watched a sports car ahead of them speed over the wet streets. "If he doesn't slow down, he's going to hydroplane. I did that once in my high school days.

Scared me to death and taught me a lesson."

Before he could take another breath, the sports car swerved to the left to avoid a huge puddle and nearly hit an oncoming car.

"Well, that was no surprise," Fred said. "The driver has his cell phone stuck to his ear. He'll either kill himself or somebody else." The car turned at the next intersection. "You're gonna wish you'd stayed back at the office."

"Oh, I'd hear complaints there, too."

"I like your sense of humor."

"We'll see if it holds when we meet up with James."

Fred pulled up in front of a new subdivision hosting upper-middle-class homes. Ryan wondered why the owner hadn't had cable installed when the house was built. Near the front, Fred pulled up next to James's van.

"I hate umbrellas, but if my wife found out I was running around in the rain, I'd be in the doghouse."

Ryan snatched up his. "I'll use mine, too."

A woman met them at the door with a toddler hanging on to each leg. "Come on in, but take your boots off. I've had enough mud tracked through my house for one day."

"Yes, ma'am," Fred said as water dripped over him while he removed his boots and balanced his umbrella. "I'm Fred Lineman, owner of Flash Communications. My foreman said you had problems, and I wanted to check on it myself."

She lifted a brow. "My husband is furious. The cable doesn't work, and the man yesterday put outlets where we didn't want them."

"I'm terribly sorry. We'll make sure the job is done right this time."

Ryan held up his shoes. "May we set these inside?"

She frowned. "Wait while I get an old towel." In the meantime water blew in on both men. When she returned, she pointed to the stairs. "The attic is in the hallway upstairs. I hope he knows what he's doing, or there will be a lawsuit." The woman looked tired.

"James is the best man I have," Fred said.

"You'd better hope he is."

Ryan observed Fred's manner in dealing with the irate woman. Nice job.

Fred and James climbed the attic stairs. "Hey, Fred. I'm about to wind up this job. It sure was a mess."

"What happened?"

"Tom didn't follow the work order. It detailed exactly what the customer wanted. That man is going to get a piece of my mind. This is the third time I've cleaned up after him."

"Let him go," Fred said quietly. "This is costing us money and making our customers unhappy. I'm surprised you haven't fired him already."

Despite the cool temperatures, sweat beaded James's brow. "He has a houseful of kids. Felt sorry for him. His wife left him, but now I understand why. Sorry, Boss. I'll tell him when we get back. The mistakes on every job were pure laziness."

Ryan filed away James's remarks. So the man had more than one soft spot in his heart.

"I'll have the customer send us the bill for any damages," Fred said.

"You sure will pay for the damages." The woman must have been standing in the hallway below the attic steps. "We've lived here less than a month, and now this."

Fred made his way to the stairs. "Ma'am, this is not the way I do business. I'm sorry for what happened, and I meant what I said. You have the holes filled and the wall painted, then send me the bill."

"I want that in writing."

"I'll get it for you now." Fred climbed down the steps, but when Ryan started to follow, James stopped him.

"I could use a hand dropping wire."

"Tell me where I should go."

James glanced up. "Don't tempt me. In the kitchen, there's an intercom system, and the wire needs to come out there."

"All right."

"I bet you've never had your hands dirty."

Ryan let the insult digest. "Told you before, I worked my way through college doing construction. Does that count?"

"It might."

"Fred told me about your little girl. Sorry to hear that."

"We don't need your pity. We got along fine before you came along, and we sure don't need you now."

Ryan bit back a retort about the possibility of two men getting fired. *He's upset about his little girl and this job.* With a deep breath to balance his temper, Ryan took the wire and helped James finish the job. After Fred made arrangements with the woman to have her walls repaired, Fred and Ryan made their way out into the rain and on to the truck.

Fred shivered. "I'm soaked to the skin. Sure glad my house sits on a hill and my wife doesn't have to get out for anything."

Ryan noted the water standing in the fields. "I wonder if I should call Alina. I'm assuming Anna is in a high and dry facility, but—"

"How do you know about Anna? I knew Alina over three years before she told me about her sister."

Ryan felt heat rise from his neck to his face. The last thing he wanted was to reveal information about Alina. He respected her privacy, and she probably wouldn't appreciate Ryan's telling Fred about their past relationship.

"You two must be getting along better than I thought." Fred threw him a sideways look.

He refused to let Fred believe he and Alina were involved. "We went to college together."

"You must have been good friends to know about Anna."

Ryan stared at the blinding rain. The windshield wipers zigzagged in front of him. *Swish. Swish.*

"Did I touch on a bad subject?" Fred asked.

"Depends on how you look at it." Why gloss over the matter? "Yeah, it's a touchy subject. We dated—we more than dated. I asked her to marry me."

Fred coughed. "No wonder she blew a gasket when she saw you. So you two were engaged?"

"For two weeks we were officially engaged. She broke it off, and we haven't spoken since. We graduated from Ohio State and went our separate ways—until now."

Fred whistled and palmed the steering wheel. "You hadn't seen her until you and I began our meetings?"

Ryan smiled. "The reunion was less than pleasant, but today she seems like the Alina I remember. I mean, friendly." His face warmed. The idea of looking like a blushing schoolboy scrolled across his mind.

Fred shook his head. "Thinking about this makes my head swim. Pardon the pun."

"Well, I'd appreciate it if you wouldn't tell her I mentioned it."

"Of course. Poor girl's had it rough taking care of Anna. . . and—"

"Being told she's losing her job by an old boyfriend?" He shook away the sensation of having a basketball lodged in his throat. He waved his hand at Fred. "Oh, I've researched that topic inside and out. God and I have had more than one discussion about it."

"He has a reason for putting you two together again."

"I told Him it would be nice if I had an advanced copy of the itinerary." Ryan's reflections about Alina bombarded his mind. "I'd like to find out how Anna's doing. It's always bothered me that her mother didn't pitch in and help with the financial care."

"Her mother died about four years ago—a stroke, if I remember correctly."

Ryan wondered if Alina had ever reconciled with her; probably not, considering her mother's unstable temperament. "How about a change of topic here?"

"Sure. What you told me stays private. Didn't mean to put you in a tough spot."

"No problem." Ryan forced a smile. "You didn't twist my arm." He surveyed the road. "Are we still heading toward the river?"

"Yes, we're on River Road. First off, I want to make sure the way to my house is not going to require oars around five o'clock. It's also a road several of the employees take. James made mention of flooding possibilities earlier."

The road swerved around a curve to a flat stretch. Water seeped over the ditches and eased across the road. On both sides of the ditches were fields that had soaked up all the rain they could hold.

"I need to call the office." Fred snatched up his cell phone. "Deidre, we have a potential problem out here on River Road heading south. It's starting to flood. Best get the word out for those who need to come this way to head on home. . . . Yeah, anyone who is concerned about flooding. Send a dispatch to the service crews, too. Their safety is more important than keeping customers happy. . . . Right. I'll talk to you on Monday."

Fred's concern for his employees was one of the differences a small cable company had over the big ones. Although Neon cared about all of its people, making money did rise to the top of the list—like the water gushing onto the road.

"Guess I'd better call the wife and see how she's faring," Fred said. "At least I have a truck."

Ryan tuned out Fred's conversation. Admittedly, Ryan felt a bit envious. The desire for a wife and family to share his life nudged him more and more all the time, but he didn't have one single prospect for Mrs. Ryan Erikson. Alina had the best qualifications, but she had this Frank guy in her corner. Sometimes Ryan felt like a lovesick schoolboy. Just when he thought he had her memory tucked away into a far corner of his heart, she stepped right back into his life. Seeing her every day was torture. The same fresh appeal that had attracted him to her in college days now held him captive again.

"See the one-story home on your right?" Fred pointed. "The one way up the hill?"

Ryan's gaze followed a winding road up to a red-brick ranch-style home. Huge oaks gathered around the front and sides, like sentinels posted to guard the master and his wife. "Very nice, Fred. I like the white fence."

"Thanks. We love it here. Makes me feel like the king of the hill. I can stand on my back patio and take in all of Radisen and the countryside. We've always opened our home to church affairs and Flash get-togethers. Behind the house is a barn with three horses, and on down the hill is a stocked fishing pond. Retirement will be good."

Ryan smiled. "Grandkids, too?"

"You bet—six of them, four girls and two boys. If you don't mind, I need to stop at the house and get my other boots. Marta will want to meet you."

An eagerness to get back to work had already attached itself to Ryan's thoughts, and meeting Fred's wife hadn't been on the day's task list—neither had the storm, the power outages, the cable problems, or the news about James's daughter. If the cable connectivity survived the day, he'd be surprised. *Patience is what I need.* "Sure. I'll probably wish I had boots before the day is over."

"Want to borrow a pair of mine?"

"No thanks."

Marta Lineman met them at the door with steaming cups of fresh coffee. Ryan expected a short, chubby woman who baked chocolate chip cookies and pulled out pictures of their grandchildren. Marta was dressed in jeans and a red sweater and stood close to six feet tall; she was blond, very slender, and looked like she must have captured every beauty queen title in the county. She welcomed Ryan as though he were an old friend. From the way she smiled at Fred, Ryan figured they must have the epitome of a good marriage. Another reason to be jealous.

"Please join us for church this Sunday," she said. "And afterward for lunch."

No doubt Fred realized why Ryan hadn't joined them for worship. The circumstances with Alina left him in an awkward situation. "Thank you. I've been attending another church here in town, but I might take you up on your offer."

"You're welcome. A couple of the other employees belong:

Deidre, Alina, and James Ferguson. Well, James doesn't belong yet, but I have high hopes."

"We've got to get going, sweetheart," Fred said once he changed his clothes and boots. "I might be home early, depending on the weather."

Marta kissed her husband good-bye. She patted his round, leathery cheek. "You bundle up good and stay dry. I don't want you coming down with a cold. Oh, I visited with Becky Ferguson and made arrangements to watch her children on Tuesday."

Ryan wanted God to bless him with a wife and a home filled with the same kind of love and affection.

thirteen

Alina had seen enough rain to last for the next year. She'd planned to get up early tomorrow morning and take Anna horseback riding at Fred and Marta's, but the weather looked to spoil it all. Even if it stopped raining this very instant, it would be days before they could set foot in the fields without sinking to their knees in mud.

She stared at the mass of options on her computer screen. For the present, she had connectivity. Her conscience told her she should be entering data and whipping out reports for Ryan, but her mind chose to wander toward him instead of his requests.

Many times she'd asked herself if the decision to abandon their relationship had really been the best. She wouldn't have had to tell him the truth about Anna, but her mother would have made sure Ryan found out. Mother's agenda centered on taking care of herself, and that meant filling Alina with guilt. But now...with Mother gone, dare she confess that her feelings for him hadn't changed? He'd want an explanation for what had happened six years ago; he deserved an answer. God clearly forbade lying—no matter what the reason. Better she deny any feelings for Ryan and stay aloof. Romance came to those who deserved the gift of love. Staying single made sense no matter what her feelings for Ryan were, and she'd resign herself to love him from a distance.

Alina blinked and attempted to focus on the screen, but her head kept nodding from lack of sleep—lack of sleep due to Ryan. What a can of worms. The door opened, and she turned to see Deidre. A worried frown replaced her friend's normal smile.

"Fred just called. Roads are flooding, and he's closing down the office early."

"Oh." Alina startled. She stood and studied the parking lot. "I can't tell a thing from here since the parking lot is often under water. You'd better go, then. I'm only minutes from home, and I can take one of the trucks if necessary."

"All right, but be careful. The weather forecast is nasty. Guess I'll see you Sunday morning." Deidre lingered in the doorway.

Alina smiled at her lovely Asian friend. "Out with it, girl-friend. What's on your mind?"

"You. I imagine you're planning to see Anna tomorrow, but if you need to talk, I'm only a phone call away. I feel bad about my visit last night."

"I appreciate you, Deidre. Things needed to be said, and we accomplished it." Alina turned and studied the continuous downpour. "I'm going to give Homeward Hills a call—make sure they're all right. That's probably silly, isn't it? I mean, the facility is up in the hills."

"Like Fred and Marta's house?"

Alina laughed. "Yes, maybe higher. Knowing Marta, she'll probably call everyone to bring sleeping bags for a party. She's probably already started the food."

"No doubt. Well, I guess I'll head home so I can pick up the kids at day care. Don't stay late, okay?"

"Me? The eternal workaholic? I'll think about it."

Deidre left her alone, and a moment later Alina learned Homeward Hills did not anticipate any problems; however, washed-out roads could be an issue for travelers. She checked the national weather site, typed in the local zip code, and saw the likelihood of more rain. As soon as the office cleared out, she'd move her car to a higher spot in the parking lot.

Fred and Ryan returned less than an hour later as the rest of the staff left for their homes; even James chose to ride out the day with his family.

"This is one time I wish I wasn't a volunteer fireman," James said. "I'll take all the snow you can shovel, but I don't mess with high water."

"Play with that little girl of yours," Fred said.

"I will. . .I will." James shook Fred's hand and punched out for the day.

With a deserted office, Alina wondered if Ryan might speak of the things Deidre had alluded to. She cringed. *Strictly business, Alina. Strictly business.*

"Are you sure you need to stay?" Fred stepped into her office with Ryan. Both dripped from the rain. "Because as soon as the last crew comes in, I'm wrapping things up and heading home to my sweet wife."

"I'm fine," Alina said. "I might as well get caught up on these reports."

"Actually, we could get a lot of work done with no one here." Ryan picked up a stack of files on his desk and turned to Fred. "But it's up to Alina. I could stay and work without her." He focused on her. "I'm leaving the decision up to you."

She glanced up at him and hoped she didn't give away her ragged emotions. "From what I heard on the radio, the electricity is out for several blocks around my apartment complex. Staying right here makes sense to me."

Fred leaned against the doorway. "All right. Promise me you two won't stay until dark. Driving through water in daylight is one thing, but trying to maneuver flooded streets in the dark is another."

"I won't let her stay late," Ryan said. "And I don't plan to either."

When Fred left, the stillness wore on her nerves. She regretted all of her earlier musings about Ryan, for now a tremendous uneasiness plagued her. She could do this. Because of him, she couldn't sleep and regularly blew her diet on chocolate and donuts. Each day that passed ticked at the countdown clock. This man not only had tormented her life for the past six years but also had torn apart her livelihood. When it came to Ryan, she made poor choices, and Alina had always prided herself on strength. Bone tired, she realized taking a nap would ensure a better disposition, but when would that happen?

"I believe I'm able to choose when it's the proper time for

me to leave the office." She wanted to argue until the sun went down. *Sleep. It must be the lack of sleep.*

Ryan acted as though her words bounced off him as off a springboard. "Of course you are."

"Don't placate me, Ryan. I don't like being told what to do."

He chuckled and continued rustling through papers. "You never have."

"What is that supposed to mean?" she asked. From the looks of his narrowed eyes, she must have succeeded in angering him. "Let me do my job and you do yours," she said. "I've never been a helpless female or an idiot. I can tell when bad weather may be dangerous." Why did she detest the sound of her own voice? She sounded like her mother. *Stop this before you regret any more words.*

"I see you're back to being defensive." Ryan powered on his laptop.

And I don't enjoy it at all. "Call it whatever you want."

"Did you have lunch?"

"No."

"Thought so."

"You are irritating me. What does lunch have to do with any of this?"

He turned his chair to face her. "I remember a few things about you, like when you don't eat, your blood sugar drops. When your blood sugar drops, you are irrational and short-tempered. So. . ." He handed her a sandwich left over from lunch. "This ought to help the situation."

Alina sucked in a breath. Not a single ugly word danced across her mind. Instead all the memories of the way Ryan had been sensitive to her needs scrolled like the credits of a favorite movie. During their college days, his kiss never failed to sweeten her up. She took the sandwich. "Thank you."

He chuckled. "You're welcome. Since we've covered the reason your disposition dropped like a bomb and handled it, I'd like your keys so I can move your car. The last I looked, the water was rising quickly."

She cringed. "I intended to move it once everyone left for the day."

"I'm already wet. No sense in you going out in it."

In a few words, he'd defused her agitation. But that was Ryan. How well she remembered. "All right. I'm a grump this afternoon. Sorry." She reached into her purse and handed him the keys. Anyone else would have told her exactly what they thought of her bitter tongue, and she'd deserve every word of it. This man was her boss. He could recommend she be fired or handle the matter himself. "Why are you so nice to me when I get ugly?"

He placed a hand on the back of her chair and bent over her. "Why not? As much as you want to pretend nothing ever happened between us, I can't." He moistened his lips. "I can respect your need for a purely professional relationship. And I will do everything within my power to try to understand when the alarms go off in your head and you lash out like I'm the enemy. If and when the time comes that I feel you're not cooperating with me in this transition, I will state so and take whatever action I feel necessary for the sake of my company."

Alina stiffened. Her heart pounded in her ears. "I understand."

"I hope so. I'm your friend." He stood and disappeared with her keys.

The rain continued to beat against the windows. Tears dampened her eyes, and she hastily blinked them back. How dare he make her cry? And he had every day since he arrived. Ryan had no right to disturb her quiet life, yet he had in every way imaginable. The old trapped feeling circled around her and pushed her farther into the corner where she had no choice but to come out fighting. She had to find a way free of this emotional entanglement, but she had no idea where to go, who to see, or what to do.

My heart keeps getting in the way. Lord, I need help. You know what I did. You know my responsibility to Anna. Dealing with Ryan is tearing me apart.

fourteen

Ryan blew out an exasperated breath. Alina's car refused to start. He pressed the hood button, then opened the door and stepped out into the cold, ankle-deep water. His umbrella provided little protection with the wind whipping it about like a kite. Once again, he felt the chill midway to his knees. He pushed away the thought of ruined shoes and new dress pants, inside which the label read: DRY-CLEAN ONLY. His mental outlook flagged while he waded to the hood. Scrutiny of the engine told him nothing more than he already surmised. *Dead battery.* Alina wasn't going to like this. She must have left her headlights on this morning.

He slammed the hood, made his way back to the driver's door, and retrieved her keys. He had serious doubts anyone would attempt to steal a car in this weather, especially one that needed a jump start. Assessing the situation, he saw no alternative but to ask Alina to steer the car while he pushed it to higher ground. A few more inches of water, and she'd be replacing the interior.

He shivered, all because he chose to play Mr. Nice Guy and help a damsel in distress. He hadn't bargained on ruining his clothes or having his feet wet and cold. An image of Marta fussing over Fred entered his mind. A little TLC might make him a little warmer inside, but fat chance Alina would oblige.

His gaze swept up an incline to where he'd parked his rental vehicle. It stood alone, but the water rose there, too. *Rain and more rain. Sure glad it takes less than ten minutes to get to the hotel.* As he surveyed the area from beneath the umbrella, he realized the parking lot and its reputation for always being under water gave him no indication about the condition of other areas of town—although from the observations he'd made less than an hour ago, he figured the water level must be rising fast. His gaze swept out to the Ohio River; nothing but flat land except for the tiny hill where Flash Communications sat. The whole area looked gray. Out in the parking lot, little gusts of wind toyed with the water. The wet wind blew in from the north and smacked him in the face, nearly taking away his breath. Living with these weather conditions permanently and by choice defied logic, in Ryan's opinion. Only a fool would consider a transfer here from sunny California.

Ryan made his way to the steps leading up to Flash. Thankfully the building stood higher than the parking lot. Even so, water splashed against the first step. By the time he and Alina locked up for the day, the parking lot would be even more difficult to exit. Once at the door, Ryan turned to take another look at the rain. He shrugged and decided to chart the storm's progress online. If the forecast grew worse, they'd leave early.

He grabbed the door handle and stepped inside to warmth. Maybe the weather report indicated an end to this mess, but glancing up at the gray sky, he saw nothing to indicate anything but more of the same. After removing his shoes and soaked socks and leaving them at the door, he wrung the water out of each pant leg and made his way back to Alina.

"Did you drown in the parking lot?" she asked without looking up from her computer screen.

"Sort of. Let's say it lived up to its reputation." He peered closer. "Blue screen?"

She blew out a sigh. "I typed in a command and presto—hosed."

"Let me take a look."

She moved aside so he could slide into her chair. After ten minutes, she offered to make fresh coffee and disappeared. Frustrated with her computer, the weather, and his cold feet, Ryan gritted his teeth and worked with the problem until the computer was restored. "Finally, success."

"I thought I was the only one who talked to my computer." Alina stood in the doorway with the most delicious-smelling coffee available to humankind. The sight of both instantly propelled him into a good mood.

"I find that most computers respond to verbal commands." He grinned. "Whatever you're charging for the coffee, I'll pay it."

"It's on the house." She placed the cups beside her computer. Steam twisted and rose, sending the aroma to his nose. Alina's sweet smile could have rivaled an angel's. And her perfume reminded him of a TV commercial in which the guy couldn't resist sweeping the girl into his arms and kissing her soundly.

She focused her attention on the screen. "By the way, thanks for fixing my computer. And thanks for moving my car."

"Correction. I tried to move your car. We have a problem," he said. "It won't start. I think it's the battery. In any event, I need you to steer while I push it to a higher spot. A little more rain, and the water will be inside your car."

She moaned and faced him. "At least I have boots." For the first time, he noted her eyes were red and puffy, and he doubted it was because of her contacts.

"You're a step ahead of me." He pointed to his bare feet, ice cube toes and all.

"Ryan, you'll have pneumonia."

"Nah. I'm too mean to get sick." He frowned. "Before we go out there, what has you so upset? If it's your computer, I have it restored. Good as new."

"I see that. Nothing's wrong. Just tired." She lifted her chin. "There should be extra boots to fit you in the service closet, maybe socks, too. The guys often change here." She snatched up her umbrella and avoided his gaze. "Let's get going."

He wanted to shake her. Just when he thought he'd penetrated her steel-encased heart, she changed moods on him. Turning her back to him, she marched down the hallway. Ryan wanted to tell her one more time that he wasn't the enemy, but why bother? Between her and James, he might as well resign himself to the fact that he'd never please either one. He managed a smile despite the situation. With the way things were progressing between them, he'd better not turn his back on her for fear he'd get whacked.

Alina's boots were made for snow and lined like a fine glove, so her feet would stay warm and dry. Ryan pushed the thought of his frozen feet aside. Once he got to his hotel tonight, he'd curl up on the sofa like an old man—and stay warm.

"In the corner is an extra pair of Fred's." She pointed to a well-worn pair of boots in the service closet. Thick socks stuck out the tops of them. "You really can't go back out into the rain with your wet shoes and socks."

Ah, so she does care a little.

Alina stopped at the glass door leading outside while Ryan pulled on Fred's boots. She gasped. "This has gotten worse. I couldn't see how fast or high the water was rising from my office window."

"Do you pray?" Ryan asked.

She slid him a curious look. "As a matter of fact, I do."

"I've been all afternoon—ever since Fred and I took a ride out on River Road. It really looked precarious with water rolling over the road. He showed me some low-lying areas where water could have easily gotten into a few homes."

"I know where that is. The people living there don't have much to begin with."

"One woman with four small children had waded to the road. Fred stopped to see if she needed help, but she said her husband had left work to pick them up."

She moistened her lips. "They all need prayer."

Both of them stared at the driving rain. He hated the thought of venturing out into the weather, and he figured Alina felt the same way. They lingered a moment longer.

"When did you become a praying man?"

"About five years ago. A friend at Neon invited me to church. I thought I was just fine, even a bit self-righteous up until that point. Anyway, every word the pastor spoke seemed to be directed at me. I kept coming back for more until I realized I needed to make a decision for Christ."

She tilted her head as though contemplating his response. "I believe it was five years ago for me, too. Mother had suffered a stroke, and Anna had a heart problem diagnosed. The combination of the two depressed me to the point that I couldn't function. Fred and Marta invited me to church. There I saw Deidre and a few other Flash employees. The first time I was so nervous and sure I'd have a miserable time that I didn't listen well to the sermon. I'd been to church other times in my life, and as a child, I learned several Bible stories." She shrugged. "I didn't understand Jesus wanted to be a part of my life. Actually, in my life. About a month later, I accepted what He'd done for me."

"I'm glad," Ryan said. "Odd, it happened to us about the same time."

She blinked. "Well, I admit I haven't acted much like a good Christian lately." She closed her eyes and released a light sigh. "Every time I apologize to you, I turn around and manage to do the same thing and behave poorly again. In any event, I don't want to discuss it any further. Guess we'd better battle this rain."

"I'm ready. When you're ready to go home, I'll take you."

She shook her head. "No thanks. I'll take one of the trucks. Once the rain ends, most of this will drain off. What's important is to get some of this work done." She stepped out under the awning and shook her head. "Like James, I prefer a snowstorm. Water scares me."

"I thought nothing ever frightened you." As soon as the words left his mouth, her face paled, and Ryan wished he could draw them back in.

"Only the big things."

"I understand exactly what you mean. We all have big things in our lives."

"Most of which are private."

Ouch. Got me there. He dreaded moving out from under the

awning and getting wet again. "Once we're out there, all I need is for you to guide your car. I'll be pushing from behind."

"Ryan, that's ludicrous. You're talking about pushing it up to a higher part of the parking lot and battling the water, too."

"I'm a strong guy. Besides, the incline is gradual."

"We need a tow truck, and I'll call one the moment we're back inside. If they're too busy in this weather to give me a hand, I'll schedule them for tomorrow."

"Might be too late."

"And I think your ego has gotten in the way of common sense." She shook her head.

"Sounds to me like you don't want to get wet." He laughed. "I'm trying to save a damsel in distress."

"The damsel has car insurance." She pressed her lips together, but he did see a faint smile. "Besides, if you drown or die of pneumonia, I'd probably be charged with murder." She opened the door and gestured for him to come inside. "Seriously, my car can be fixed or replaced. Your health and safety aren't worth the risk."

"Thanks. Let's not bury ourselves in work to the point we aren't watching the weather." He helped her slip out of her coat. When he touched her shoulder, they both jumped. *Junior high kids.* "Let's finish the data run and call it quits."

"Agreed." She glanced around them. "I don't relish the idea of spending the night here anyway."

"Oh? Why not? We could talk about old times."

Alina frowned as her boots tapped down the hall. He'd made her angry again.

fifteen

Alina clicked PRINT, heard the printer kick into gear, then watched it spit out the ten-page summary showing Flash's accounts in varying graphs. All the while, the rain beat against the window, and her mind kept yanking her back to the spring of her twenty-first birthday. Her junior year of college was nearly over with a wonderful summer ahead teasing her senses. She had Ryan, and love had taken over her heart. All the misery of the past seemed to fade when they were together. If it hadn't been for him, her studies surely would have slipped, but he insisted they do their best. Alina clung to his every word as tightly as she clung to him. He had a great future ahead of him, and he wanted them together to enjoy every moment of it. Ryan talked of marriage as readily as he spoke of their grand summer—and her birthday. She remembered walking across campus. The snow had melted to slush, a not-so-pretty sight when the pure whiteness of winter mixed with mud, but it promised the showers of spring and beautiful growing things. Like her love for Ryan.

"What do you want for your birthday?" Ryan held her hand tightly, his leather jacket thrown over his shoulder. How handsome he looked. How much the other girls envied her.

"Just you." She laughed at her whimsical words.

"No, that doesn't work. I need a definite."

She held her breath, thinking an answer would soon fill her head. "I honestly can't think of a thing."

"This is dangerous, because now I have to use my imagination."

"Surprise me." Anything he chose promised to make her life

112

even more wonderful. She should have told him how her life now had meaning with him, but she refrained, feeling a little foolish about making the confession.

Two weeks later, on her birthday, he stopped by the apartment she shared with two other girls. He carried roses in one hand and a teddy bear in the other.

"Flowers and a teddy bear, how sweet." She inhaled the sweet scent of the flowers.

"Oh, the bear isn't for you," he said. "I thought we'd take it to Anna and spend the day with her. I have a cake in the trunk with party hats, birthday plates, and napkins."

Alina cried. He understood exactly what made her happy. Nothing could ever separate them. Their love meant so much to her, and to see him include Anna in his plans demonstrated the depth of his feelings.

In one year's time, everything changed.

Alina gathered up the pages from the printer and set them on Ryan's desk.

He looked up, his light blue eyes captured her gaze, and the feelings she vowed to hide surfaced again. Her stomach fluttered.

"Do you remember the frat party when we dressed as Dorothy and the Tin Man?"

He's remembering, too. "Vaguely." *Of course I do.*

"You carried a stuffed dog, and I roasted in the Tin Man suit."

She tried to remain dispassionate, but the memories coaxed her like a warm fire on a cold evening. "Weren't we planning to go as Luke Skywalker and Princess Leia, but couldn't find the costumes?"

"Yeah, we waited too long and somebody else beat us to them. I do remember we could have gone as Yoda and C-3PO, except my pride refused to let me walk around all night with Yoda's ears." Ryan eased back in his chair. "We were good together, Alina."

She turned back to her desk, but the cherished part of their past longed to be revisited. If she said one more word, she'd cry, and the tears might never stop.

"I'm sorry," he said. "That wasn't fair."

Alina's thoughts had already slipped back. She walked down the hall to the ladies' room. At least there she'd have privacy to recall the music and laughter, and what Ryan had said to her the night of her birthday. And if she chose to drown in the liquid emotion, well, that was her business.

"I love you, Alina," Ryan had said. "Nothing will change that, and because I feel this way, I'll always put you first in my life. We're together for life."

She'd leaned against his chest in the front seat of his Mustang and listened to the pounding of his heart.

Alina made it to the ladies' room just before she broke into a flood of tears. If she'd stayed in her office with Ryan much longer, he'd have asked why she broke off the engagement. And in her present mood, she might have hinted at the truth.

Blinking back the wetness, Alina blew her nose and studied her face in the mirror. Swollen eyes and splotchy skin wouldn't win a beauty contest. At least Ryan had been polite and not asked why she'd been crying. Perhaps a glimpse at the parking lot might interrupt her self-pity. She blew her nose again and tossed the soggy tissue into the trash. Great—rain drenched the outside world, and her tears drowned the inside. She opened the door and walked to the back of the building.

Nothing had prepared her for the sight: Water had risen midway up her car. Alina gasped. Earlier she'd cast away any worries about damage to her car, but viewing it made her short of ill. She'd purchased it less than two years ago, and she had one more year of payments left. Her gaze swung to Ryan's leased SUV, and its wheels were almost covered with water.

"Is it worse?" Ryan asked as he made his way toward her. He must have been watching the ladies' room door and seen her exit.

"Yes, steadily rising. My car is about to get a seat full of water, and yours is not far behind. I wish a tow truck could help us."

"You said the line was busy?"

She nodded. "Makes me wonder if some phone lines are out."

"Did you try more than one business?"

"Sure did. I thought they were all out helping people caught in the rain." Her stomach twisted with fear.

"I am so stupid, utterly stupid," Ryan said. "We should have left with the others, but no, I wanted to work." He gestured toward the outside. "Now I'm wondering how you'll get home and I'll get to the hotel."

"One of the service trucks?" She noted the water making its way up the tires.

"We can try, but first let's call the police department and see what the streets are like."

"And I'll log on to check the weather, too," she said. "I turned the radio off earlier—it was interrupting my concentration. Looks like I needed to be interrupted."

The lights flickered, and the hum of the office equipment faded. Utter silence swept over her.

"There it goes," Ryan said. "Sure glad my laptop has a good battery, but I'd venture to say our Internet connectivity is probably gone, too."

The conditions outside suddenly looked more menacing with the loss of power. The streets had to look better than the parking lot, and she did have a second-story apartment in a relatively high area. But first she had to get there. "I'll get a set of truck keys so we can leave as soon as you find out which streets are passable."

He nodded and jogged back to the office.

"The phone book is in the bottom right-hand drawer of my desk," she said.

"Got it."

It only took a moment to grab a set of keys from the service pegs. Her mood had ventured toward the dreariness she saw outside. Rather than watch it rain, she made her way back to her office. She observed Ryan standing by his desk, one foot propped on his chair. His casual stance eased her trepidation and the turmoil swirling through her head.

"Yes, Flash Communications on McKinley Street. I'm wondering how the streets are around us, because the parking lot and everything around us look to be flooded." Ryan nodded while the other person spoke. "So if it looks too dangerous, sit tight. Should I call back? We are in a rather isolated area. . . . I understand. Thanks."

Alina hadn't realized she'd been holding her breath, but she released it the moment he put the phone back on the cradle. "We're supposed to sit tight?"

"Some of the streets aren't passable, but we can probably get through most of them in one of the trucks. If that doesn't work, then I'll call them back, and they'll send someone after us."

"As in a boat?"

"Exactly." He smiled, but she found no humor in the situation. "I suggest we get our things and try to make it out of here."

As soon as Ryan powered down his laptop and grabbed up a handful of papers to stuff in his computer case, they braved the weather again.

Outside, Alina studied the water reaching the second step. Without a doubt, she was frightened. The area from Flash to the river looked like a solid sheet of water. Her apartment sounded like a slice of heaven. She handed Ryan the truck keys.

"I don't want to try driving."

His eyes narrowed. "You're trembling, Alina. I'm sure we'll do fine once we get going." He chuckled, but she could tell he forced it. "Too bad Fred doesn't own an amphibious vehicle." He took her arm and guided her down the steps. "The water is cold, and it's going to get into your boots. My advice is not to think about it." He lifted his computer case above his head. When he couldn't manage the case, the umbrella, and Alina, he left the umbrella behind.

Her first step deeper than the height of her boots shocked her system. "Oh!" She shuddered.

"I know, but the truck isn't that far." The calm, in-control inflection of his voice soothed her a bit. She could do this. How many times had she told herself the same thing over the past few weeks? They had to move fast, because the longer they delayed, the less likely it was they'd make it home. She refused to think of the late afternoon shadows darkening around them.

"Ryan, the water is like stepping into an ice bucket, and it feels like I'm being pelted by mini icicles."

"Really, Alina, has anyone ever thrown icicles at you? Tell me how that feels." He reached for her hand, and she wrapped her fingers around his.

She understood he wanted her to talk and not think—and Ryan had protected her in the past. *Lord, I'm terrified. Please help us. You know I can't swim.* "It's like when I sprained my ankle two years ago and I had to keep my foot in ice. At the time I thought the ice was worse than the pain."

"See, I walked through this earlier. My feet haven't thawed out yet, so this is a piece of cake."

"How nice."

"Focus your eyes on the truck. It *is* getting closer."

She wanted to cry. No wonder all those people from the *Titanic* drowned. The idea of "hypothermia" written on her death certificate didn't sit well. "I'm trying to be optimistic."

"Good. I'm proud of you."

"Will the truck even start?"

"I'm praying about that."

"Me, too." She tightened her grip on his hand and prayed.

"There is one consolation," he said. "If this was the middle of summer, we'd be sharing this water with snakes."

"Oh, Ryan, you always were able to find the humorous side of things."

"All but one."

Alina didn't reply. She knew exactly what he referred to. Just as her legs threatened to grow numb, they reached the hood of the truck on the driver's side.

"Crawl across from my side," Ryan said. He opened the door to find that water hadn't gotten inside.

"Normally I complain about climbing up into these things," she said. "But not today."

Ryan gave her a boost up, and she crawled across the seat and over the gearshift. Once seated on the passenger side, she took his computer case and placed it on her lap.

"I never thought dry could feel so good," he said. "Now, to get this baby started and out of here." He inserted the key, and the engine sang into action. "Yahoo!" he shouted.

Alina clapped her hands. "I feel like a kid at Christmas." Her gaze swept around them. Water everywhere. She shivered but kept her reservations to herself. At least the thunder and lightning had ceased.

sixteen

Friday, 5:15 p.m.

Ryan inched the truck backward. He didn't dare go forward; the parking lot sank deeper in front of them. He took a quick glance in the rearview mirror and saw that the lines across his forehead resembled a plowed field. He fought the water while he straightened the truck. "Here we go. Lord, we need all the help we can get."

"I'm not so sure I can tell where the parking lot ends and the road begins. Be careful. There are deep ditches on both sides."

Ryan eased to the highest point of the parking lot, then turned the truck toward what he believed was the road, giving himself plenty of room for error. The likelihood of them making it to safety looked slim, but he wouldn't tell Alina. The dips in the streets were like water retention ponds. Oars. . .he needed oars.

The truck inched ahead and onto the street. He flipped on the heat, grateful the vehicle's engine hadn't cooled too much since its crew parked it. The welcomed warmth boosted his confidence. His gaze followed to the top of a hill. If the truck made it there, he could evaluate their position. At the crest, Ryan stared out at the gray-shadowed streets below. Everywhere was water—and rising. Behind them looked like a small lake. Before them appeared to be an extension of the river. The few vehicles stranded along the street were nearly submerged. With late afternoon fading to evening, the world around them held a sinister chill.

"We can't risk this," he said. "We'll have to turn around."

"I know," she whispered. "We're better off inside Flash."

He didn't want to comment on waiting at Flash for a boat

to rescue them. Right now, he had to get Alina back on dry ground, and he had no experience in driving through water except the commonsense factor to proceed slowly. Uneasiness crept over him as he considered how to turn around without sinking into the ditch. *Lord, if You wanted my attention, You have it. I'm scared. Help me turn this truck around.*

Ryan pressed his foot onto the clutch and slipped the gearshift into reverse. He gripped the steering wheel like a kid taking his first driving lesson. Alina stared at him, her face a ghastly shade of white.

"I'm not afraid of dying," she said through quivering lips. "But I always thought drowning would be one of my least favorite ways."

"I'll do my best to keep those fears unfounded." He wanted to say more. He even wanted to reach over and squeeze her hand. Tell her she'd be okay. Instead he offered a tight-lipped smile.

His goal was to stay in the same spot on the road and slowly turn the truck around by alternating between reverse and first gears. It sounded good in theory. Maybe if he owned a boat, he could figure out the maneuverability.

His head pounded, and his ears filled with the sound of moving water. The slow battle to head the truck back to Flash consumed his senses. The windshield wipers sailed back and forth. The evening moved in faster. . .darker. Alina gasped, but he didn't have time to give her attention.

"I'm afraid to look and afraid not to," she said.

"If you think I'm getting too close to the ditch, speak up."

A crack of thunder startled her. He well remembered her fear of storms. The truck finally made its 180-degree turn and moved in the direction of the parking lot. He felt his shoulders relax. "Don't care to try that again." Lightning raced across the darkening sky. How would he get her out of the truck and into the building in an electrical storm? In the past, she refused to drink water or walk past a window during a storm.

"Ryan, I have never been this scared."

It may get worse. "I know you are. Soon we'll be back inside the building and on the phone to the police."

"But I am getting warm. How nice it would be if our clothes were dry and the electricity was—"

He glanced her way and forced a smile. The engine sputtered. He caught his breath. In the next moment, the engine died. He turned the key. Nothing. He tried again. Silence.

"We have to walk, don't we?" Her voice quivered.

The thought of looking at her frightened expression was more than he could handle. "I'll help you."

She reached for the door handle. "I'm sorry about all this."

"Why? How could you have known?" He tossed a confused look her way.

"I could have gone home earlier and eliminated the whole mess."

"Alina, I'd have stayed and worked alone. No matter how you look at our situation, I still would have been here. And if you think about it, I should apologize to you for not insisting that you leave with Fred."

She said nothing but opened the door. The water slapped against the side of the truck. Thunder rumbled, and she instantly pulled the door shut. Terror shone in her eyes.

"We have to do this," he said. "We cannot stay in the truck." He remembered years ago when Alina had become ill during a severe thunderstorm. "I'm going to come around and get you. I don't want you falling." He spoke slowly, wanting her to grasp every word.

"Don't—don't forget your computer."

"I managed it before, and I will again." He refused to comment that his laptop might not make it to the building. Right now, he wasn't so sure they would.

"And you have a plan?"

The defeat in Alina's voice alarmed him. She was frightened. And so was he. "Let's pray first." He reached for her hand and lowered his head. "Lord, we're surrounded by water, and we need to make it back to the building. Daylight is fading, and a storm is closing in. You know all the obstacles against us, but I want to remind You. Go before us, Lord. We need You." He glanced up at her. "I'm not poetic when it comes to prayer. I tell Him how I feel and ask for guidance."

She nodded. "It was...perfect. I'll wait until you come around."

Ryan opened the truck door, dreading the initial step. As his boots filled with water, he sank to midcalf. The cold water nearly took his breath away. He gritted his teeth while clutching the computer bag. "This isn't bad." By the time he made his way to the passenger side, she'd opened the door and appeared ready to attempt the trek to the building.

"Let's hurry, please." Lightning flashed across the sky, followed by a crash of thunder.

In the short time it took for her to utter those words, Ryan realized nothing mattered but to get her to safety. He tossed the computer bag onto the truck seat and grabbed her hand. "I'll come back for this later. We'll make it, Alina. I promise you." *Lord, help me to keep this promise.*

Hand in hand, they waded through the water over the road. He kept his sights on the two-story brick building, and his fingers wrapped around Alina's. "Talk to me. Tell me, what's the first thing you'll do when we get back to Flash?"

"Thank God for keeping us safe and peel off these wet clothes." Her teeth chattered.

"Do you have an extra set?"

"No, but the service people usually do. We—we both will need to change."

"Then what will you do?"

"I'll probably want to cry because of this horrible mess we're in, but I'll do my best not to."

He smiled. "I don't mind. Maybe I'll cry with you."

"Real men cry?" she asked.

"Absolutely." Ryan remembered what losing her had done to him. Yes, real men wept buckets when they were upset.

The evening shadows spread, signaling the imminent cloak

of darkness. His gaze swept from right to left; if only he knew for certain where the ditches bordered the road. A wrong step could prove disastrous. An image of water covering their heads and washing them down the street formed in his mind.

"I hate electrical storms." Alina's voice bordered on hysteria.

"I know." He squeezed her hand a bit tighter. "Think back to what your dad used to do when you were afraid."

"I'm surprised you remember, but he sat me on his lap and held me tight."

"Picture God doing the same thing. There's no need to be afraid. He has you within His fingertips."

"You haven't forgotten a thing, have you?" she asked.

"I hope not. Memories were all I had left of you." He stopped himself before he said more.

"I wonder if we had known God back then, if things might have turned out differently," she said.

We have God now. What's stopping us? "We can't go back, Alina. We can only look to the future."

The journey seemed to take forever. He weighed the gravity of crossing the road, knowing that falling into the depth of the ditch could be their demise. The shadows played tricks on his memory, and with the power outage, his sense of direction became distorted. This must be what complete trust was all about.

The storm sounded closer, like a dog on their heels. One more step. One more step. In the ever-darkening sky, the lightning lit a brighter path above them. Alina whimpered. He would carry her if she wanted him to. She stumbled, and he righted her before she fell. Their umbrella did little good, for the wind twisted it and turned it inside out.

"We're close," he said. "It won't be long now."

At last their feet touched on the building's concrete steps. Ryan wrapped his arm around her waist and helped her to the door. He opened it wide.

"I forgot to lock it." She muffled a sob. "And I'm so glad."

He squeezed her waist lightly, and she stiffened. Not much

had changed, but this time frustration surfaced.

"Does it bother you that much for me to touch you?"

"What do you mean?"

"You know exactly what I mean. When you were afraid to step out of the truck, I wasn't repulsive. And when the thunder and lightning caused you to nearly fall, my hand must have felt pretty good, because you didn't let go." He recognized his harsh words were from stress, but he didn't stop them. "Sometimes I wonder if you're human."

seventeen

He's right. How can I be so insensitive? Alina fought the urge to let Ryan hold her. He had every right to be furious with her. One minute she warmed up to him, and the next she treated him like last week's trash. She wanted to admit her feelings for him, even if they could never be together. She wanted his strong arms around her while the angry water swirled outside. Without Ryan she'd still be sitting in the service van, slowly drowning while thunder and lightning paralyzed her.

Ryan peered out at the inclement weather. "Alina, I'm sorry. I was way out of line."

"No, you were right. I'm fickle. Thank you for getting us back here. I mean, you could have left me back there, and who would blame you?" Her words were surely nothing more than pathetic hot air to the man who had saved her life.

He whirled around in the shadows. "We're a matched pair, Alina. Neither one of us has the guts to admit we still care for each other." His shoulders lifted and fell. "Better take off those boots."

She started to move toward him, but fear of what that meant yanked her back into reality. She would only hurt him when this ended. Tears pooled in her eyes. Were her tears for the man she loved, or were they for herself? She shivered and bent to remove the boots and socks with cold, trembling fingers.

"Alina, I'm sorry for tearing into you like that."

"I heard you the first time. Let it alone. It's over." She pulled off her wet socks. "We aren't the same people."

Ryan opened the door and dumped the water from his boots. He took hers and did the same. Both of them stood shivering in their bare feet.

"I think I can find us some dry clothes," she said.

"And I'll call the police." Ryan disappeared down the hall. Her feet hurt from the cold, but she had a job to do. Inside the utility closet, she hoped to find everything they needed, even dry socks. A distinct chill had taken over her body and seemingly numbed every part of her. In the dark, she rummaged through all the paraphernalia belonging to the service people until she wrapped her hands around a pair of jeans and then another. *Socks. Surely there is a pair here.* Alina crawled around on the floor of the closet until she had searched every square inch. When she found none, she sat back against the wall, willing her tears to stop. She had better control of her emotions than this.

No socks, but she found one pair of boots, two pairs of jeans, a lined coat, a couple of sweatshirts, and a towel that smelled of engine oil. After piling them on the floor outside the closet, she searched for flashlights and found three of them. Alina gathered up her treasures and headed to where she believed Ryan had disappeared. She promised herself to be cordial to him. Ryan leaned against the doorjamb.

"Are the police on their way?" she asked.

"Not exactly."

Her heart plummeted. "What's wrong? What did they say?"

"The phone's dead."

"But we have our cell phones."

"I can't get through on either of them. And naturally there's no Internet service."

She wanted to see his eyes, for there lay the truth of their plight. "We're in bad shape, aren't we?"

"I'm sure we'll think of something. We're out of the weather, and yes, we're without power and communication. Looks like the generator finally ran out of gas, which means the two-way radios don't work either. But things could be a lot worse." He glanced around them. "I'll get Fred's radio from his office. I want to keep up-to-date on the weather and see what emergency procedures are in place to help those stranded."

She pulled the clothing articles closer to her, and one of the boots fell. "I guess we're in for the night."

"Maybe not." He retrieved the fallen boot. "I'm not giving up on a rescue team until we're dry and warm."

The lump in her throat felt like a baseball. "I have a few things we can use. These boots are for you."

"And you?"

"Oh, I have what I need." At least she could be a little unselfish with this mess. She handed him a pair of the jeans and a flashlight. "These should fit and are most likely a little big, but anything is better than standing here in these wet clothes. The rest of these will help us bundle up as the night wears on."

"Thanks." He took the items and moved toward the men's room. "Didn't find any sleeping bags, kerosene lanterns, or dry towels?"

"I wish. We'll be all right until morning. A little chilly maybe, but these coats and sweatshirts will help." She moistened her lips and wished she felt as optimistic as she tried to project. "We could look upstairs, too, although mostly equipment is stored up there. Oh, the break room has a few supplies."

"Extra batteries for the flashlights and Fred's radio would be nice. Say, are you hungry?"

"Starved. There's food in the break room," she said. "Let's change and look for a little supper." She had to take charge of her emotions. Do something, anything to keep her mind off the weather and the water.

"Alina. . .thanks."

The lump in her throat grew to mammoth proportions. "No problem."

Once she got out of her wet slacks and secured Fred's radio, she met Ryan in the hall. She gave him the radio and tightened her belt on the men's jeans that must have been twenty sizes bigger than her waist. But they were dry and they hung below her feet. He'd not see her bare feet unless he shined a flashlight on her. "I think I got the bigger pair." She tried to laugh, but the sound seemed more like the whimper of a sad puppy.

"Do you want to trade?" he asked.

Thunder shook the building.

"Nope. These are mine, and I'll manage just fine, thank you." Hopefully her response sounded light and didn't betray the terror rising in her faster than the floodwaters outside.

They made their way to the break room. Fumbling around in the dark with only the aid of a flashlight gave her an eerie feeling, even with Ryan alongside her. *Later on tonight or in the morning, we'll be rescued. I'll never take electricity for granted again. Never.* The long night loomed ahead.

She aimed the flashlight toward a drawer in the kitchenette. Inside lay a package of matches, candles, two packages of batteries, and two light sticks. Whoever had been in charge of equipping the break room had included a candleholder. She'd buy them a steak dinner when life got back to normal. With the strike of a match, the candle lit the small room just enough to switch off the flashlights.

"I think," she began as she opened the cabinet above the counter, "we have a lantern." She pulled it off the shelf, then set it down beside the candle and switched it on. "I rather like dining by candlelight, and the lantern may come in handy later."

Ryan sorted through the supplies. "I wonder if there are any six-volt batteries in here." He opened the cabinet door and found two batteries. "Jackpot." He flipped on the radio, which was tuned in to a station out of Cincinnati. Not exactly what they needed. He played with the tuning dial until a station came in clear and crisp.

"Radisen has been the hardest hit by the flash floods. The rains continue, and rising water has forced most of the town to higher ground. The downtown and east-side areas already have several homes and businesses under water. Fortunately, emergency personnel state that the downtown area has been completely evacuated."

"No, we haven't been rescued!" Alina sucked in a breath to

still her ragged emotions. She forced her attention to hear the rest of the news report.

"Emergency officials warn residents who are in dry areas and higher elevations to stay at home. Roads are washed away, and two deaths have been reported due to the flooding. One woman employed at Radisen Bank drowned when she took an elevator down to the parking garage and water rushed through the door. The Red Cross has set up shelters at Radisen High School and First Methodist Church on Adams Street. If you are near a flooded area, secure higher ground. I repeat, secure higher ground. Water has reached second-floor levels in some low-lying areas. Many individuals have volunteered boats to help find stranded victims. Phone and power outages are reported in and around Radisen. The weather forecast says more rain through tomorrow. Stay tuned for updates."

"I can't swim," she said.

"What?"

"I said I can't swim. So if you're thinking that is a way out of here, you're on your own. I simply can't go out there again."

"Alina, trying to swim to safety would be foolhardy." He paused for a moment. In the flickering candlelight, she saw the sadness on his face and bit back the urge to weep. "I didn't know you couldn't swim. Doesn't matter anyway; I'm not about to leave you stranded. We'll be rescued. Remember, I talked to the police department and told them we were here. It's a matter of time before someone knocks at the door and escorts us out." With a smile, he wagged his finger at her. "Where is your optimism?"

"But they think everyone on this side of town has been evacuated." Her lips quivered. Didn't she just tell herself to be stronger? "I'm whining. I'm so sorry. This isn't your fault."

"We both would like to blame someone or something, but the truth is we're in this together. I don't have any answers." He shrugged. "Let's get something to eat; then we can talk about what our next move should be."

Alina recognized the calmness in his voice, an echo from

years before. Lashing out at him solved nothing. His words were meant to pacify her mounting anxiety. "You're probably right. Fred keeps the refrigerator stocked."

She pulled out sodas, lunch meat, cheese, fruit, and bread. Paper plates, napkins, and cups rested on the end of the countertop along with a bag of corn chips. A few moments later, they took turns warming their hands over the candle.

"This feels so good that I hate to stop to fix my sandwich," Ryan said.

"I agree, but my stomach has been grumbling for hours—and you've witnessed what happens when my blood sugar drops."

"Go ahead and make yours. I'll keep the fire stoked."

She made sandwiches for both of them in silence and brought them to a small table.

"Thank you. How about I bless," he said.

"Go ahead; and you can mention our predicament, too." She bowed her head.

Ryan took her hand. He didn't ask permission, but she wasn't about to create another scene. "Father God, we thank You for bringing us back here safely. We ask that You send a rescue team and keep all those safe who are in danger this night. Thank You for this food and for this shelter. Amen." He gave her hand a gentle squeeze and released it.

"I never thought bologna and cheese could smell so good," she finally said.

He bit into his sandwich. "Or taste as good as a steak dinner."

She broke off the bread crust and tossed it in the trash. "They now make a crustless bread."

"I bet you save hours of time." He chuckled, and it broke the tension. "Here I thought you'd outgrown the habit."

"I still remember your lectures about all the vitamins in the crust. You even talked to a nutrition expert about it."

"And I still remember your response: 'I'd rather swallow a vitamin.'"

She smiled; it seemed to come from her heart to her lips. Time ceased to exist in a few captivating moments. Sensing her emotions soaring beyond her control, Alina turned from his gaze.

"It was good then, Alina. We didn't have the Lord, but He had given us the gift of love."

She laid her sandwich on the paper plate. A myriad of responses whisked across her mind, but nothing she dared say.

"I understand," he said after a moment's silence. "Perhaps it's enough for us to be friends."

The radio repeated the same news interspersed with country-western music. The electrical storm had faded into the distance, but the relentless rain and wind continued to pound against the building. Her fears consumed her. A whole night at Flash, in the dark, with Ryan? What purpose did God have in trapping them in a building surrounded by water? She questioned whether the turmoil outside the building matched the upheaval in her heart. Better to let humor disguise her anguish than to go with honesty.

"I think I know how Noah felt," she said. "Claustrophobia must have been a biggie."

"Look at it this way. We don't have to feed any animals. . .find the snakes that wiggled out of their cages. . .walk the tigers. . .or find out if anyone is playing hide-and-seek with the monkeys."

She laughed at the whimsical image. "Do you ever wonder how they cleaned the stalls?"

He wrinkled his nose. "I never thought about it, but I'm sure you have."

"It's crossed my mind, especially if it all piled up."

"God had it all worked out."

"Like us?" She reached for a corn chip.

"I'm certain of His plan, and it's reassuring, too."

"I feel bad for the woman who was trapped in the elevator— makes it hard to trust God when tragic things happen." *Like Anna. Dear, sweet Anna.* "And I hope all the other employees are high and dry."

"But, Alina, we don't have a choice. As followers of Christ, we know the flip side of not believing in His almighty hand."

She nodded. "I'm afraid, really afraid, but I'm glad you're here with me—another Christian." She bit into her sandwich.

"This may be the reason we're together," Ryan said. "We'll have to wait and see."

When Ryan finished at Flash and they went their separate ways, she'd look back on this evening and cherish the closeness. A haunting image kept piercing her thoughts. "Do you think the building will flood?"

Ryan glanced above the candlelight. Lines had been added to his face since the morning. "It's a strong possibility."

She dropped her sandwich and nearly knocked over her soda can. "What will we do?"

He paused. "Guess we'll simply head up to the second floor, but I hate to think of our companies dealing with damaged flooring or losing some of the equipment." His eyebrows lowered.

"What are you thinking, Ryan? What should we do?"

"My thoughts are we have no idea when rescue efforts will reach us. In the meantime, I want to carry computers and any other equipment upstairs. Files, too."

She picked up her napkin and whisked away crumbs from her hands. "I'm ready to help. Fred deserves more than to have everything he's worked for destroyed, even if it belongs to Neon now. I understand insurance pays for catastrophes, but I want to do all I can. Sitting here and waiting will drive me crazy."

Ryan stood from his chair. "Why don't you begin by taking some of this food upstairs—and anything else you can think of. Who knows how long we'll be here."

"Sure. As soon as I'm finished with that, I'll help you carry equipment to the second floor."

He snatched up a flashlight and disappeared. She took a deep breath, certain her frenzied nerves would encourage the contents of her stomach to come back up. That was a possibility she'd rather not consider. Closing her eyes, she prayed for strength and courage—and a quick rescue.

Alina had seen a paper bag in the drawer. First she snatched up the matches, candles, batteries, light sticks, and paper towels. Atop those items, she put the fruit, cheese, meat, bread, and chips. She'd gather up the water bottles on the next trip.

Ryan suddenly appeared in the doorway. "Hurry, Alina. Water is coming in the front and back doors."

eighteen

Ryan left Alina in the break room and went to move all he could upstairs. His fears concerned not only the first floor but the second one as well. With no end to the rain in sight, Flash Communications held no barrier to the rising water. He prayed a rescue team would park their boat outside the building long before Alina learned the precariousness of their circumstances.

He grabbed an extra flashlight, then the clothing items she'd found. He also gathered up their wet clothes. But by the time he started up the stairs, he wondered why. It would take a long time for them to dry, and he hoped to be far from Flash Communications before then.

His vision fought to adjust to the second floor's darkness. Even with the flashlight teetering atop his load, he kept bumping into one thing after another. He knew desks and file cabinets divided up the area, but he hadn't memorized where. Finally he set it all down and turned on the lantern. With the extra batteries, they were in good shape. He simply didn't want Alina in complete darkness when they were finally forced upstairs.

Once he divided up the items, he hurried back down for Fred's equipment. His office was nearest the door; it would be the first to receive water damage. In his mind, a list began to form of computers and paper files taking priority. His boots sank into rapidly rising water. *Time, Lord; I need time.*

Alina appeared in Fred's office with her hands full. "Unless you give me a list, I'm taking what I feel is important," she said.

"Do what you think is best." Ryan unplugged Fred's

computer and wound up the cord. "I wish we had blankets. I'm worried about you getting sick."

"I'll be fine." Alina adjusted the load in her arms. "My head is swimming. . ." She obviously checked herself for what she'd said. "Ryan, I've never been so frightened."

"I understand. Another reason for us to keep busy."

"We can't get everything upstairs in time." Desperation nudged at her words. "I'm not whining, just feeling helpless."

He opened desk drawers and pulled out various files he thought were important. The flashlight shined on a picture of Marta and two other photos that must have been Fred's kids and grandkids. He lifted the computer into his arms and piled the papers and photos from the desk drawers on top. "Pray. All we can do is our best. God will honor our efforts."

She expelled a heavy sigh. "You know, it's a blessing Fred isn't here with his heart problems. Marta told me in confidence about the seriousness of his condition."

"You're right. He told me his heart needed some repair work. Anyway, we youngsters can handle this until help arrives." Ryan no more felt like being humorous than he wanted to swim to safety. But if he admitted his well-founded fears, Alina would be hysterical.

"I hope so. I pray so." She turned and disappeared into the dark hallway, and in another moment he maneuvered his way toward the back stairway.

"Alina," he called, "grab the radio and bring the files left on our desks." He remembered the important files stuffed in his computer bag, no doubt floating in the service truck by now. Some of those documents should have been shredded, but little good his observation did now. Another thought needled at him. At the first sign of possible flooding, Neon executives should have received a call advising them of the situation here. Instead he'd underestimated the danger. His actions would not look good on his next performance evaluation.

Mr. Independence, his family had labeled him. "Can't tell him a thing," his mother had said.

"If Ryan doesn't have the answer to something, he'll not own up to it," his little brother said last Christmas when the family thought he'd gone for extra firewood. "I don't like talking to him about a college major or my plans for a career, because he has all the answers and isn't interested in what I have to say."

Admittedly so, Ryan prided himself on being in control—almost to the point of using manipulation. Not a thing to be proud of. If he'd learned one lesson today, it was that God held the title of knowing all the answers and possessing all the control. As he sloshed through the water, it occurred to him that this lesson had been a hard one to learn.

Lord, forgive me for my arrogance. My family needs a Christian man who listens with both ears and not with his ego. If I'm given the opportunity, I'll apologize and do a better job of pleasing You.

For the next forty-five minutes, the two managed to carry several computers, three printers, a fax machine, and other valuable equipment to the second floor. All the while water seeped in beneath the doors, reminding him of the perils all around them. Ryan and Alina battled nature and a river that climbed its banks like a huge sea monster longing to escape the trenches of the deep. He pushed the image from his mind. Later when they were safe, he'd internalize the meaning of today's events and the way he intended to let the day impact his life forever.

He heard Alina splashing her way toward him. Odd how her boots made different sounds than his. "How are your arms holding out?" He carried a small filing cabinet by Deidre's desk.

"Doesn't matter," she said. He heard her open a cabinet in their office.

"Don't worry about those files in the top drawer. They've been entered in the database and backed up at the home office."

"What about the second drawer?"

"We need all of them, if possible. Concentrate on the paper trails, and don't try to lift any more of the equipment. You'll hurt your back—and then I'll have to carry you." She had to be exhausted, and humor looked like the only way to slow her down.

"I'm okay, really. Must be adrenaline tearing through me, and banging around masks the thunder."

He hadn't paid attention to the weather outside. "One storm after another must be passing through. I feel sorry for those out in boats looking for trapped victims."

"I think I could handle almost anything but standing in water during an electrical storm. Somebody would have to give me a valium injection—triple dose." She laughed, but Ryan heard the trepidation in her voice. She glanced around. "When we're rescued, we could face what I just said."

"Oh, you'll be so glad we're heading for dry ground, it won't matter." He recalled the way she used to ask questions when she was nervous or upset. His Alina—how well he knew her habits.

"What happens to the buyout if a lot of these things are damaged?"

"The deal's done," Ryan said. "All of Flash belongs to Neon."

"Then Fred's been paid?"

"Yes, but the business is managed jointly with Neon until the end of the transition period."

She nodded. "I see. We're helping both companies by transporting equipment and files upstairs."

"Right. But, my dear tiger woman, let me emphasize that neither company wants you hurt in the process. By the way, are your feet thawed?"

"Hmm, about the same."

"When you take this load upstairs, why don't you take a break? Pull off those boots and wrap your feet in a couple of those sweatshirts."

"I'll consider it in a little while."

"As your boss, I'm ordering you to make an effort to get warm."

"Ah, but I'm a stubborn woman."

He didn't comment. No need to.

❧

Alina watched Ryan disappear up the stairs with Deidre's file cabinet. She had slipped to a state of vulnerability with him. How easy it would be to confess her heart. How easy it would be to tell him he'd matured into a wonderful man and a capable executive. How easy it would be to tell him she remembered every moment of their two years together—to tell him she loved him with her whole heart. How easy. . . Shrugging away the misery accompanying her musings, Alina lifted out the files from the second drawer of her file cabinet and laid them in a cardboard box. She'd located two boxes in a storeroom and used them to carry the files upstairs, unload them, and repeat the process. The idea of stumbling to the wet floor and soaking the files Ryan needed for the transition bothered her—bothered her a lot. After all, she'd made a commitment to do her best in the three-month process. Already, she had a positive nibble on her résumé—a Columbus pipe company needed someone with a solid computer background. She'd schedule a follow-up on Monday, along with recruiting a headhunter to help out in the job search. Job security meant the time remaining with Flash would pass by more positively.

Conviction moved her to center her prayers on all the others who could be equally devastated by layoffs. She had a problem of self-centeredness, not exactly a characteristic she relished.

"Alina, you are the most giving person I know," Deidre once told her. "You care for Anna not only with your time but with your money. And look at what you do for others at Flash. Birthday cakes for everyone. Perky cards that take time to select. When it's raining you bring in donuts. My kids love your chocolate chip cookies. No, you are not self-centered."

Alina could have listed the selfishness oozing from her being, like the times she avoided James because she thought he was a redneck, or avoided the servicemen after a hard day's work because they smelled of sweat, or avoided Jackie in the new-order department because she snapped her gum while she spoke. "Condescension" was not listed as a spiritual gift. And then she had picky eating habits and refused to patronize some restaurants, often causing awkward situations with friends. The list went on and on.

Lord, I'm not trying to bargain here, but when Ryan and I are rescued, I'll do a better job of serving You. Today has proven how quickly life and the things of earth can be snatched away. This world may not be as I'd like it, but it is what You planned for me.

She hoisted the box of files into her arms. At first, the water spread over the tile beneath her feet, freezing her toes. Now her feet were numb, and the soaked pant legs of her jeans dragged heavily. The water level circled above her calves, and she found it harder and harder to move. A quick glimpse at the lighted dial on her watch showed that the water was rising much faster than in the beginning. She and Ryan raced against time.

Her ears had seemingly grown accustomed to the pounding rain outside. It needed to stop before more people were hurt and property destroyed. For the moment, the storms had subsided.

Ryan's shadow emerged from the doorway. "Have you tried your cell phone lately? Maybe it's working." The confident timbre in his voice gave her a little more strength.

She handed him the box and retrieved her phone from her jeans pocket. She pressed 911, but no voice greeted her, only a busy tone. "Nothing," she said. "I'll keep trying."

Ryan had yet to find out she had nothing on her feet, not that it mattered now, since the water splashed at her knees. Pushing aside the discomfort, she pulled out another drawer and set it on her desk before the water reached the files. She'd removed the bottom drawer only a few minutes before. Soon they'd have to climb to higher ground. When she considered all the equipment about to float, she forced her frozen legs and tired arms into action for one more load.

Come Monday, when Fred and Ryan phoned the insurance company, she'd pride herself on these heroic attempts—even if they benefited Neon Interchange.

"I'll take my load back." She reached for the box. "I'm growing real attached to these files."

"And when you deposit it upstairs, take a break before I wrap those legs and feet myself."

She laughed and ignored him. He'd have a fit when he learned she wasn't wearing shoes or socks.

nineteen

Ryan finally realized the futility of this ridiculous attempt to move the lower office up to the second floor. Although he'd condemned his power-control efforts and inability to admit defeat, he still carried armloads up the stairs. This had to be a way to ward off insanity. And what of Alina? What strange bacteria or virus could she contract in these murky waters, besides pneumonia? He'd dump this load and demand they stop, demand they end this foolish escapade.

He cringed. *God, why is this happening? The flood? With Alina? What are You wanting me to learn?*

"I don't want you falling, and carrying all this stuff through this deep water is going to cause you to lose your balance." His voice echoed through the building.

"Tough. I'm determined. It's after working hours, if you hadn't noticed."

He smiled despite their circumstances and waded toward the doorway. "Know what?"

A drawer slammed shut. "I haven't a clue."

"If I had to be with anyone tonight, I'm glad it's you," Ryan said.

"So you have plans of us drowning together?"

"Nope. I have plans of us being rescued together."

"Thanks for the clarification."

"Hey," he said, "did you remember to get the bottled water?"

"It made one of the first trips upstairs, but if you're not picky, dip your cup anywhere around. Drink at your own risk."

A crash sent a streak of fear through him. "Alina?"

Nothing.

141

"Alina?"

Bile rose to his throat, and his heart thudded against his chest. He couldn't get to her fast enough. "Alina." His flashlight first found her legs, then her upper torso. She lay against his desk, her head leaning dangerously close to the water. A file drawer balanced on her chest. With an unprecedented display of strength, he heaved the drawer onto the floor and swept her up into his arms. "Say something, Alina. Oh, I'm so sorry. I shouldn't have involved you in this stupid stunt."

She moaned. "I'm. . .all right. Just stunned."

He passed through the water with his sights on the steps. "Where are you hurt?"

"Banged my head. Fell backward."

He couldn't hold her and shine the flashlight at the same time to see the extent of her injuries. "It's time we hit the high and dry floor."

"I'm. . .sorry."

"Hush. This is Ryan, the guy who—" *has loved you for eight years.* "The guy who is the head of this operation." He managed to lay his flashlight atop her, and she held it in place while he floundered through the water and up the stairs.

"Ryan."

"Hush. There's no need to talk."

"I have to say this."

His heart sped into overdrive. Had she broken a bone? Internal injuries? "Are you sure it can't wait until later?"

"No it can't. I'll change my mind." Long moments passed before she stirred. "About back then. . . You weren't to blame. It was nothing you did."

He bent and kissed the top of her forehead. The thought of her swatting him with the flashlight crossed his mind, but he didn't care. For six years he'd fretted over what he'd done to cause their breakup. In less than ten seconds, the years of worry vanished. "Thank you."

At the top of the stairs, he laid her on the carpet. "Wish we had a sofa or a blanket here." The lantern light rested beside a couple of sweatshirts, and he snatched them up—not sure what to do with them since her clothes were wringing wet. He angled the flashlight to the right of her face. "Show me where you hit your head."

She touched the back of her head, near the crown. "Ouch. I feel a little knot."

"Anyplace else? Your back? I don't see any blood." He felt the spot where she complained. A huge lump had already formed. He'd read somewhere that was good—no lumps after a fall signaled a concussion for sure. "I'm going to get some ice."

"I'm sure I'm fine."

"What's one more trip to the break room? I might find some leftover donuts while I'm there."

"I do have a request. See if there are any other clothing items left hanging in the utility closet. We both are soaked."

"Got it." He left her and hurried down the steps. Each trip he made to the first floor brought a few more inches of water, and the rain continued to pelt against the windows. No wonder the businesses and homes in the lower elevations had flooded to the second floor. By now those same places could be covered to the roof peaks. He gulped. Once he had Alina settled, he'd look for a way to get to the roof. He remembered having the light sticks, but something told him to wait awhile longer, although the nudging made no sense. *Lord, keep Alina safe and rescue us.*

In the utility room, Ryan found a greasy pair of coveralls that most likely belonged to Fred. The garment would cover the man's two-hundred-pound frame; it would swallow hers. He'd change into the coveralls and give her what he had on—except his pant legs were wet, too. Nothing else remained. Everything else she'd already taken upstairs. Gathering up the ice into a towel, he made his way back to Alina. Water topped the second step. *Seeping in like a predatory animal.*

Her eyes were closed, and the sight of her alarmed him. He needed to shine the flashlight over the rest of her for blood. Her jeans needed to come off and probably the shirt, too, and he hoped she fared well enough to complete the task.

"Let me take a look at the rest of you." He pointed the flashlight beam at her feet. "Alina! Where are your boots?"

"Surprise," she whispered. "I only found one pair in the closet, and they weren't my size."

Fury raced through his veins. "You are worse than a child. I can't believe you did this."

She propped herself up on her elbows. "Nothing you can do about it now."

"We've got to find a way to get you warm." He shined the flashlight near her face. Pale. She could be in shock, and all he knew was to wrap her in blankets, which they didn't have.

"This is not how I planned things," she said. "I wanted a medal of honor from Neon and a management position here in Radisen." She laughed, but it sounded pitiful. "A raise and a new car, clothing allowance. . ."

He forced a smile. He had to stay calm to keep her calm. "If you had orchestrated tonight, I'd be a little concerned about your mental condition. I found these coveralls, but they're huge and smell like grease."

"Probably Fred's."

"The same."

"Good. I can wrap up twice and be comfy cozy. This is no time for me to be picky. Mind if I use one of the sweatshirts?"

"Knowing your habit of hiding things, I'm checking through all the things you brought up for a clean pair of socks." He rummaged through the hodgepodge of foodstuff and supplies from the kitchen until he realized she hadn't lied about the socks. "Can you change by yourself, or do you need my help?"

"I can manage, if you can escort me to the ladies' room."

One more time, he picked her up.

"Really, this isn't necessary," she said.

"Why don't you save your strength? The night is young. In fact, I'm still so furious that it's better you say nothing. I might drop you."

"A little bump on the head doesn't make me an invalid."

"Given your judgment of what is necessary and what isn't, I'll call the shots from here on out."

"Just exactly what you do best."

She'd nailed him with the one trait he detested most about himself, but he refused to back down. He intended to take care of her whether she liked it or not.

Alina took so long to change that he banged on the door several times to make sure she hadn't fainted. When she did emerge, she clung to the door and wall. Without waiting for her to protest, he carried her back to the spot near the lantern.

"Do not move. I'm heading down to see if there is anything else we might need. Promise me you will stay glued to this spot."

She turned her head away from him.

"I could tie you up."

"All right. I get the message."

❧

Saturday, 12:15 a.m.

Alina turned off the flashlight while Ryan traipsed through the first floor. No point in wasting batteries. She shivered. She'd never known such depth of cold—crying cold, made-her-want-to-scream cold. Dry clothes had helped, and she refused to complain. Ryan had done all he could to make her comfortable, and she recognized his old zeal to fix the world's problems.

The pain in her head hammered away each time her heart beat, and like an obedient child, she held the ice pack in place. A half dozen Tylenol sounded good, and she had a bottle of them in the bag from the break room. Changing clothes had taken forever: First she feared getting physically sick; then she nearly fainted. She wanted to close her eyes, sleep for hours, but with a banged-up head, she knew that wasn't smart. *Lord, I pray I don't have a concussion. I'm already depending too much on Ryan.*

Fear seized her, and she closed her eyes against the nightmarish thoughts racing through her brain. If she and

Ryan didn't make it through the night, who would take care of Anna? Who would visit Anna and take the time to brush her hair and roll her wheelchair out into the sunshine? Who would point out the butterflies with their colorful wingspan and pick flowers for Anna to smell? Who would hold her when life frightened her? Granted, Anna was the beneficiary on Alina's life insurance policies, but money didn't buy love and devotion. *Oh, Lord, keep my precious sister safe. May there always be someone to love her.*

A tear trickled down her cheek. She needed to be stronger. After she took two Tylenol and the ice reduced the size of the lump on the back of her head, she'd think clearly again. Timidity and failure had never characterized Alina, and she shoved away the thought of falling to them now.

She eased back onto the carpeted floor with the ice firmly against her head. Weariness made her long to take refuge within the sweet confines of blissful sleep. In an unconscious state, she wouldn't have to think about the flooding, her feelings for Ryan, Anna, or her job situation. She shook her head to put some life into her body. *I can't sleep. I need to help Ryan.* Memories danced across her mind, beautiful days with Ryan. Slowly her thoughts swung to the many regrets. . .Anna's accident. . .Mom's disappointment. . .breaking the engagement with Ryan. . .the years of loneliness. She understood God had forgiven her sins, but the reminders lived with her like a cancer that slowly enveloped her life.

Joy had settled in her life in three ways: her acceptance of what Jesus Christ had done for her, the love she felt for Ryan, and the precious moments she shared with Anna. God had not abandoned her, but the knowledge did nothing to stop the insidious reminders that she might not live to see her sister or Ryan again. Taking a deep breath, she gave in to the tugging at her eyelids.

twenty

The water had risen to slightly above Ryan's waist. Too cold for any human. Even his bones ached. Why hadn't he changed back into his wet dress pants? Stupidity. Mr. Executive blows his itinerary. Foreboding nipped at his heels. The water rose as though a spigot had been turned on high. If it continued at this rate, it would reach the second floor long before the light of morning. Wading through this mess made no sense. He needed to check on Alina.

He'd found nothing on this trip—a sure sign not to enter the murky kingdom again. Thunder rumbled. He could only imagine Alina's hysterics if they needed to plop themselves on the roof in the midst of an electrical storm.

Once he mounted the steps, he called out for Alina. Nothing. "Alina."

When no response met his ears, panic shook him. He hurried to her side, desperate to see if she could be roused and yet cautious not to drip water on her. "Alina, wake up." *Lord, please, we don't need a serious head injury.* He nudged her gently, all the while calling her name. He shined the flashlight near her face; the ice packet lay beneath her head. Deathly still. Her coloring hadn't improved. Cavernous pits, deep enough to hide in, lay beneath her eyes.

"I'm. . .I'm awake," she said.

He blew out a ragged breath. "You scared me."

"I'm tired, Ryan. Sorry. Didn't mean to frighten you."

"How long have you been asleep?"

"Not sure." She yawned. "You think I have a concussion?"

"Crossed my mind." *More than once.*

"Remember, I'm a morning person, and it's probably after midnight." Her words were slurred, but she was coherent. "This lump is a problem only if you can't awaken me." She closed her eyes. "Can I sleep a little longer?"

"I suppose." He wanted her awake and sitting up—complaining, teasing, anything but sending jabs of alarm across his mind. He peered into her face and fought the urge to pull her into his arms. "Keep in mind I'm going to nudge you every hour."

"Go right ahead. Anything else, Doc?"

"Yes. Where's the entrance to the roof?"

"Did you hear a helicopter?"

No, sweetheart, but I hear thunder. "I want to be ready."

She pointed behind them. "There's a door in the right-hand corner that leads up a few steps to the roof.

"Okay. Got it. You rest, and I'll do some exploring."

Snatching up a flashlight, the radio, and the light sticks, he walked to the right corner and found the door.

Locked.

Alina had left her personal keys by the paper sack full of foodstuff. He couldn't think of a single reason why she'd have the key, but he prayed she did. Once he retrieved her keys, he attempted to open the door with every key on her ring. None of them fit.

Plan B.

"Superhero" had never been listed on Ryan's résumé as one of his attributes, but desperation had a way of manufacturing muscles and determination. Standing back from the door, he took a deep breath. Praise God it wasn't steel. Various TV and movie scenes flashed before his eyes. Of course they all had cardboard doors or stuntmen to handle the obstacles. He kicked it hard. The force shook it but did little else. With his borrowed steel-toed boots, he planned to do much more damage than the slight indentation. He kicked again. And again. Why did everything have to be so hard?

"Ryan, what's wrong?" Her weak voice spurred on his resolve.

"The door's locked. Unless you have a key, I'm playing the role of superhero."

She moaned. "No, I don't, and I have no idea where to find one."

"Never mind. I'll get it open my way."

Ryan's frustration over the past several hours suddenly manifested itself in an all-out assault on the door. He kicked at it with a force that surprised him, nearly shattering his foot. For a moment he wondered if he'd broken it. *Use a chair, Superman.*

With renewed determination, he grabbed a chair and slammed its steel legs into the door, not once but several times. Finally he successfully made a hole. Reaching inside, he twisted the knob.

"It's open," he said more loudly than necessary, but the echo inched up his confidence level and hopefully kept Alina awake.

Ryan set the radio inside the door, then made his way up eight steps to where an access panel lifted up to the roof. The rain pelted him like sharp needles. How long could this keep up? Lightning flashed. His and Alina's conversation about Noah took on more vivid form, except Noah didn't have rising water on the first floor. He preferred looking for wayward snakes. Taking care of Alina and applying some humor to the situation might help him from going crazy, but he was scared and not too proud to admit it.

Ryan held the access door as a break from the wind and rain. His gaze swept in all directions, pitch black and no signs of emergency boats or helicopters. Ryan recalled the news: All of the people on this side of town had been evacuated. Why would anyone think to search for two people trapped in a building? Every few minutes the same weather report repeated with the same updates. Surely someone would have reported them missing. What about the call he'd made hours ago to the police station? Ryan clenched his fists. Panic only served to freeze up his thought processes and show a lack of trust in God.

God colored the big picture on a canvas too vast for Ryan to conceive. He purposed the outcome of this nightmare, and He didn't need to file a missing person report. If death came in the hours ahead and heaven awaited them in the near future, how bad could that be? God knew exactly where they were, and His promises were the biggest comfort of all.

He grasped the umbrella and flashlight in one hand and climbed onto the roof. The access door crashed shut behind him, much like a clap of thunder. Alone on the roof with nature's fury whipping around him, Ryan felt an eerie sensation veil him. While God orchestrated His creation in sights and sounds that could shake the mightiest of men, He also provided shelter. Bits and pieces of Scripture took on new meaning, strengthening Ryan's faith in a supernatural display of profound assurance of God's provisions. A blast of wind lashed through Ryan and sent him to his knees on the wet roof. The umbrella flipped inside out. The flashlight soared ten feet ahead. Lightning flashed above his head in a jagged streak. The sensation stole his breath. Yet a cloak of peace fell over him with such intensity that he wept aloud.

"My God, You and You alone are in control. Take away my pride and let me see only Your glory."

Ear-piercing thunder shook the roof, and Ryan trembled. *Be still, and know that I am God.*

Time proved irrelevant as Ryan listened to the roar around him, but the terror subsided. With its dissipation, he sensed the courage to face whatever lay ahead.

Ryan stood and studied the malevolent sky. Rain poured on his face and offered a liquid stream of unfathomable joy in a dimension he would never be able to express. For certain, he'd treasure this communion until he met the Lord face-to-face.

He twisted the light sticks guaranteed to glow for several hours. One on each end of the roof would draw attention. Dawn would come around six thirty, and with morning came the expectation of someone finding them. He rested in the hope of light drawing out rescue workers to search for stranded victims once again.

Ryan climbed down into the small stairwell. He needed a few

more moments alone before confronting Alina about a matter. Whatever lay in the future, sin festered in their past. Ignoring the black mountain between them didn't make it disappear.

He flipped on the radio, although weather updates had been more of the same. A woeful song blared out about a man sitting alone in a bar. It ended, and another one began. If he never heard another country-western song again, he'd count it a blessing. Reality was not emotion-based but God-based.

News broke into the music. "Here's the latest update on the flood situation in Radisen and the surrounding community. Rescue attempts are in progress for those stranded by the deluge flooding south-central Ohio. Where once local emergency officials believed everyone had found safety, the unrelenting rain has forced them out of their homes. Two more people have drowned in the wake of this torrential downpour, which brings our numbers to five deaths since yesterday afternoon. Various reports of missing persons have rescuers scanning the area. A late report confirms a volunteer was killed when struck by lightning. If you are in a danger zone, seek higher ground immediately. The governor has declared the south-central Ohio River region a disaster area."

Big deal. What good is an official declaration? He lowered the volume. Helplessness inched through the pores of his skin. He sensed doubt prying at the doors of his heart. Prayer seemed so minute when he'd always been a man of purpose and action, yet the awe of God's provision gripped him again.

His muscles ached from carrying equipment up the stairs. His back felt like someone had used it as a punching bag. Ignoring the stabs of pain, he pulled himself up from the step to check on Alina. The inevitable waited for him. Even if she refused to discuss the issue between them, he'd state the truth. He walked past her sleeping form to the stairs and shined the light downward; the water had reached within a foot of the first floor's ceiling. No blaring trumpets, just a steady rise, a still, deep killer.

No point in putting it off any longer.

twenty-one

Alina inched up from the serenity of deep sleep. She fought the waking. Luscious, sun-filled days enclosed her dream world, a safe place. One she didn't want to leave. Anna laughed, called her name. Someone called Alina's name. She stirred.

"Hey, sunshine," Ryan said. "How's the lump?"

"Much better, thanks to your ice pack."

He gingerly lifted her head and lightly touched the back of it. "That's my girl, but from the size of that knot, you're stretching the truth again." She heard the smile in his voice. Love swelled in her heart for a man she could never call her own. The bleak circumstances surrounding them failed to stop those deep-rooted emotions, the ones she dared not confess.

Alina tried to sit up despite the pounding in her head. "I'd concede to one more Tylenol and a bottle of water. They're beside the paper bag." She watched Ryan stumble about in his wet clothes. "Wouldn't your dress slacks be more comfortable than those?"

He handed her the Tylenol and twisted the lid off the water bottle. "I think I'll change. These coveralls feel like I'm carrying an extra fifty pounds. As soon as I'm finished, I'd like to talk."

"What about?" She glanced toward the stairway. "The water's rising faster than you thought, isn't it?"

He glanced back and nodded. "We have a lot to discuss."

She lay down and closed her eyes for a few minutes more. When she opened them again, she saw Ryan on his knees. The flickering candlelight lit up his silhouette: head bowed, hands clasped together in a tight fist. *He's praying. The rain hasn't stopped. He must believe we're destined to die.*

"Ryan, let me pray with you. Don't carry this burden alone."

"I'm not. God has the biggest load. Go ahead and pray for us. I've bent His ear long enough. Your voice is sweeter than my raspy attempts at getting His attention."

Although Ryan's sense of humor surfaced in the turmoil, panic seized her, and she swallowed hard. "Father God, thank You for keeping us safe. You've provided food, clothing, and supplies for us tonight. You've also given us shelter, and we're grateful. We ask for You to send help. We pray for all those who are alone and frightened in this storm. Give them peace and the assurance of Your loving hand. Your Word assures us You will never leave or forsake us. Thank You." Alina sobbed and fought to regain her composure. "Thank You that Ryan is here with me, and I don't have to face the rest of the night without another Christian. In Jesus' name, amen."

The rain remained a steady sound. Any other time, the rhythmic flow would have lulled her to sleep. No thunder. No streaks of lightning. How deceptive.

"How much of the first floor is immersed?" She tried to mask the apprehension in her spirit.

"It's nearing the top."

Alina gasped. "What time is it?"

"About three."

"We're not going to make it, are we?"

He walked to her side and knelt down. "We have God, Alina. We both prayed, and it's all we can do in the spiritual department. I don't mean to sound disrespectful." He shook his head. "I believe daylight is our key to getting rescued. In the meantime, I lit the light sticks on the roof."

She shivered and wrapped her arms around her. "When you kicked the door in to get access to the roof, it was because of this—not just the light sticks."

"I imagine we'll end up there before long."

She was glad for the shadows around them. At least he couldn't see her fright.

"Alina, I want us to talk a moment."

"About what?" Surely he didn't plan to interrogate her about what happened to their engagement.

"We did not honor God back then."

She stiffened, determined to leave the past behind. "I wish you hadn't brought up our. . . It's easier to forget without a reminder."

"But you haven't forgotten, have you? We thought love gave us a license to act like we were married. I'm sorry. I shouldn't have pushed you." He peered into her face as though expecting her to respond. If he chose to talk about what they'd done back then, he'd have a solo conversation. "More importantly, I should have put God first."

"We weren't Christians then." Her heart raced. "I asked God for forgiveness."

"So did I, but I never apologized to you."

"It's not necessary, but thanks. Ryan, we aren't the same people today. Put it behind you. Go on with your life. You've confessed it to God and apologized to me. Nothing's left."

"Why are you bitter?"

"I'm not." She swallowed. Her head hurt, and she shrugged. "Perhaps I'm a little bitter." *I'm in love with you and have more regrets than I care to admit.* "God may have brought us here tonight for closure. My fault. . . I'm sorry about all the things I did to upset God and hurt you."

There, she'd said it. "I meant every word, Ryan. What I did was inexcusable, but both of us need to move forward. I'm doing it." *What a lie.* "Now please tell me about our predicament here." She hated doing this to him.

He clenched his fist. "We need to gather up what we need and move to the stairwell."

"Then wait for the water to rise there?"

"You got it. We're racing against time and daylight. Plus the light sticks are an added bonus."

"I'm frightened." Another confession. "And I'm trusting God, but it doesn't end the panic."

"Does it help to know I feel the same way?"

She offered a nervous smile, for to speak would invite tears that would drown out any words. His admittance of fear melted her resolve to stay aloof, even if death loomed in the next few hours.

Ryan kneeled and drew her into his arms. Leaning against his chest, she closed her eyes and sobbed for several long moments. "I'm such a coward. I prayed, and now I cry."

"You're wrong. Look at how hard this afternoon and night have been, and you've done just fine. I believe we'll get out of here."

"I hope so. You always had a way with words, making me feel like things were better than they were."

"Glad I still have the knack."

He held her tightly, and she relished being held in his strong arms. "You are God's messenger tonight," she said.

"There are many things I could say, but I'm not sure God wants them said."

"What do you mean?"

He sighed. "Does your head still hurt?"

"The Tylenol has helped. You haven't answered my question."

"It's hard."

And she understood that he hadn't stopped loving her. She'd seen it in his eyes the moment they were alone in her office. "I'm not so sure I'm ready to hear what you have to say. I do wish things had been different."

"Me, too. Lots of times."

"You want to know why," she said. When silence met Alina's ears, a force stronger than her will prompted her to forge ahead. She'd vowed to keep those things locked in her heart until now. "I wanted to explain, but it's all very ugly."

"You were a private person." He kissed the top of her head. She didn't mind. For a few moments, she could indulge herself in remembering how it used to be between them.

"Guess I've been more open with you than anyone else,

although I've talked to Deidre about some things about us." She grew warm. "Not everything."

"So what did you do, plan a lynching?"

She smiled, snuggling against his chest. "Not exactly. She read into my frustration the moment I told her we'd dated in college. And I told her about the first time you met my mother."

He chuckled. "That was classic."

She moistened her lips. Her gaze swept to the stairway where the lantern cast a shadow to the water gleaming wickedly a short distance away from them.

"Don't look at the water."

"Still reading my thoughts?"

"Of course. It has a long way to rise before the roof."

She knew his words were meant to comfort her. Right now she had her own storm raging against her soul. Being nestled against his chest gave *security* a whole new meaning and spurred her on to reveal the truth.

"Tell me, Alina. I've waited six years to find out what changed your mind."

If they died this night, did it make any difference? Except he'd push her away. But Deidre would say that sharing the burden was supposed to lighten the load. "I need to explain the situation about Anna and my responsibility to her. I accepted her care a long time ago." She hesitated. Her head pounded.

"I remember in college you worked to help take care of her," he said.

"There's more to my commitment than the love I feel for her. It's—it's my fault she's mentally challenged."

Curiosity, woven with sadness, deepened around his eyes.

"Anna was born as normal and alive as we are. She and I used to chatter like a couple of little chipmunks." Alina closed her eyes. "We played and got into all kinds of trouble until we were three, when she had an accident."

"You don't have to tell me this unless you want to," he said. "My days of pushing you into situations are over."

"But I must. It's why I broke our engagement." He squeezed her lightly, and she relished the affection, knowing in a few moments he'd be repulsed. "When Anna and I were three years old, Mom took us to a department store in Columbus. I wanted to play among the ladies' dresses. I liked hiding my face in the folds of the skirts, but Mom insisted we stay right by her side. I saw a round rack of ladies' robes and wanted to run across the aisle. I whispered to Anna to follow me." She took a deep breath. "I slipped away, but Anna hesitated. When she decided to join me, a mirror fell from the ceiling on top of her."

Ryan's hold did not waver. "And you blame yourself for her accident? Hasn't anyone ever told you it was the store's neglect?" Indignation laced his words.

"Mom didn't see it quite that way. She said *I* coerced Anna to follow me. If I had listened to her and behaved, Anna wouldn't have suffered all these years. From then on, Mom blamed me for Anna's handicap. I hadn't obeyed, and God punished me by letting Anna get hurt. Mom never let me forget and reinforced the punishment by saying that I had to take care of my sister until the day I died."

"That isn't fair! She had no right to saddle you with unwarranted responsibility." He said nothing for a few moments. "Now I understand the animosity between you and your mother. Whenever I heard her criticize you, I wanted to demand why. Maybe I should have." He gently massaged her arm. "Surely you don't believe Anna's accident was your fault."

She tilted her head. "Yes. . .and no. I disobeyed my mother, but I repented of my sin. God forgave me, but I don't think Mom ever did. She went to her grave claiming I was responsible for Anna's handicap. There are no relatives alive who visit Anna, and Dad died while we were very young. My point is that I can't ever ask anyone to take me into their life—and Anna, too—especially with what I did."

"That's why you broke our engagement?"

She nodded. "Mom said I shouldn't burden you with my problems. She said if I didn't end the relationship, she'd tell you the truth."

"And you believed her?" His voice rose. "What about how I felt?"

She pulled away from his stiffened body. The anger she'd feared seeing in him all along now surfaced. "I'm sorry, but I love Anna. Caring for her is not a duty or an obligation; it's a joy."

"I'm not upset about your love for her, nor your desire to make sure she's taken care of properly. I admire your commitment to Anna."

Confusion clouded her logic. "What do you mean?"

"I expected her to be a part of our lives one day. I'm angry because you believed your mother. She had no right to judge how I felt about the matter any more than she had a right to judge you as responsible for the accident." A crack of thunder shook the building. She shuddered, and he took her hand. "Alina, I've never stopped loving you."

Alina froze, paralyzed by what she'd heard. Ryan's words whisked away the years of doubt and misery that had almost consumed her life. Afraid to move or utter a sound for fear he'd deny his love for her, she struggled for the right words.

"Why, at the point when it looks like our lives are to be swept away, must we finally learn the truth?" she asked. "I've never stopped loving you either."

He rested his head atop hers. "God has been dealing with misunderstandings and two stubborn people."

"And I'm the worst. You always gave unselfishly to me."

"Not always. At times I manipulated you. I thought you believed the rumors about me and Jenny."

"The cheerleader who needed help with her French? Never gave it a thought once you explained. You told me about tutoring her, and I trusted you." She lifted her face to him. "Ryan, we've wasted years that we could have been together."

"We have these moments, for as long as God allows." He

paused. "I think we needed this time apart to grow in the Lord."

"I used to be afraid of God, because all I knew about Him was what I heard my mother say. Fear and repulsion confronted me every time someone mentioned His name. When I realized His heart was full of love for me, I embraced His love like a child running into the arms of a father."

"I turned to God when my life no longer made any sense."

His ardent gaze swept over her face. Even in the dim light, the warmth in his blue eyes penetrated her soul. He lowered his head and kissed her lightly, brushing his lips across hers in featherlike softness.

"Do you mind?" he asked.

"Please do. I've waited a long time."

His kiss became a promise fulfilled. The years vanished along with the hurt and the sadness. His love soothed her doubt and regret like a gentle balm. Bittersweet emotions caused tears to flow unchecked over her cheeks. She didn't care. If the waters overtook them this very instant, she'd die knowing the truth had sweetened the moment.

"Alina, tonight you've given me a taste of heaven. God is so very good."

Suddenly the ironic circumstance of their meeting held clarity. She swiped at her tears. "God also has a sense of humor. Not only did He put us back together, but look how He got my attention. We had to work side by side in a job transition that I despised, and then you had to inform me of not having a job at the end of three months. The only reason I stayed this afternoon when Fred sent everyone else home was to give you a bad time—to prove I was committed to Flash."

"I suspected your tactics. Selfish me wanted you alone in the hope that something from the past might be rekindled. I failed to consider the weather would turn out like this."

A beep interrupted him.

"My cell phone," she said. "It needs to be recharged—like my poor heart."

He kissed her cheek. "I have my phone off. Every so often I turn it on to see if I can use it."

She picked up a flashlight and aimed it at the stairway. "Look. The water is seeping over the top."

twenty-two

Ryan hated the thought of a slow death, and he intended to fight it all the way. "We'll go higher as the water rises. I'll get a few things to take with us."

"I want to help."

"What about the lump on your head?"

"I'm fine."

When she started to get up, he reached under her arm and righted her. He then watched her to make sure she didn't topple over. "Give yourself a few minutes before you attempt anything."

Alina made her way to the items brought from the break room and pulled out a plastic garbage bag. She proceeded to put some of the foodstuff inside, along with extra batteries and a first aid kit. Her sideways glance at the staircase stabbed at Ryan's heart. *She can't swim, and she's petrified of electrical storms. Lord, please deliver us.*

"I'll take those." He took the bag and led Alina to the stairwell. She seemed strangely quiet, not her usual manner of handling stress. "It's less than three hours 'til dawn. We'll make it."

"Thanks. Of course we will."

Once she sat on a step, he opened the access door leading to the roof and pushed up to see the outside. The wind blew water across the roof and into his face. The light sticks looked to take flight at any moment, and the temperature had dropped since he'd checked earlier. They'd be shivering before long. He counted about six feet before they needed to move onto the roof. Every foot bought time. The old cliché about it being the

161

darkest just before dawn rolled across his mind. They were in a war zone, and the enemy might not have had grenades and high-powered rifles, but it had the advantage. He refused to give up. He had faith and a God who answered prayers.

But what if death came before sunrise? All of his ponderings started and ended with the same question. He remembered the apostle Paul and his conviction that living was good but dying and being with Jesus were even better. Ryan felt the same way, but that didn't mean he and Alina planned to take a dive into the first floor.

Am I ready to meet Him? While he sat on the steps, the faces of all those he treasured drifted through his mind—along with what he should have done differently. His parents were in their late fifties, healthy, traveling, and active in church. How often did he call or visit? And his sister in Oregon and his little brother attending Ohio State? Holidays and birthdays didn't cut it. While traveling, Ryan often hadn't bothered to look for a place to worship on Sundays—he could have sacrificed and been more involved no matter where he was. *I could have shown others Jesus in me. God, if You will only get us out of this mess, I'll—*

Ryan startled. He refused to make a bargain with God. If he and Alina survived, he committed to making changes. How sad that a catastrophe had to bring him to reflections about himself. Alina's voice broke into his ponderings.

"What is it?" he asked.

"The water's here."

❧

Saturday, 4:15 a.m.

Alina leaned against Ryan's shoulder while they shared a coat and a sweatshirt. She tried not to shiver. He'd always been one to "fix" things when she'd been uncomfortable, and he had plenty to concern himself with now—without any more problems. She recalled a time just before she broke up with Ryan when he'd found her crying. Alina couldn't tell him how her mother had berated her for considering marriage.

"I can't help you if you won't tell me what upset you," he'd said.

"It's my mother. We had a disagreement."

He'd frowned. "Anything I can do?"

"No. This is a difference of opinion." And her mother had won. Two weeks later, Alina broke their engagement.

In the dark and seated on the fourth step with their heads nearly touching the access door, she slipped her hand into his. A candle offered a faint light as it burned near the base of the wick, sending a halo effect on the step beneath them.

"I'm being philosophical here," she said, pointing to the candle. "But I'm thinking this small circle of light is like our legacy."

"And what will we leave behind?"

She half-laughed. "Nothing earth-shattering for me. I wanted to make a difference in the world, especially after I became a Christian. I thought of taking mission trips or sponsoring orphans overseas. All I've ever done is volunteer in the nursery at church."

"You took care of babies?"

"Yes, I did, Mr. Erikson." She lifted her chin and forced a smile. "Why are you so surprised?"

"Not surprised. Pleased. And I'm sure those parents appreciated it. So you've left a fine legacy. Me, that's another story. I have a fistful of regrets when it comes to my family. I've always been too busy to give them my time. Earlier I was thinking about what I wish I'd done differently. I almost did the barter thing with God. You know, 'I'll do this if You'll rescue us.' As soon as the thought entered my mind, I realized how that mind-set lowers God to human level."

"You are a fine man, Ryan. Always have been, and you gave so much of yourself in our relationship. When we're rescued, I pray I never forget how precious life is and how important every human is to God. I want my legacy to give God a smile. He knows my weaknesses. I could have been less sarcastic and more courteous to others. I could have taken time to understand people like James." A picture of James rolled across her mind—his anger, his interest in the things of God, and his little daughter's illness.

"He's a hard man to understand, and I hope God is able to get through to him."

"He made life miserable for you, didn't he? You never said a word."

Ryan shrugged. "Doesn't really matter. I want to believe that by not blaming him, I made a difference."

"He's searching."

"True, like all of us."

She squeezed his hand. "If given the opportunity, I will strive to make a difference."

"Do I fit into those aspirations?"

She smiled. "Do you want to?"

"For as long as God allows."

"Sounds like you have serious plans."

"Just listen to my plans and give me your opinion. I see a cloudless day in June, after the Flash/Neon transition. The sun is shining warm, birds are singing, and flowers are blooming everywhere. A limo pulls up in front of your red-brick church. The driver exits and opens the door for you. And you, Miss Alina, are dressed in white and carrying red and white roses. You walk up the steps to the church entrance. You pause for a moment and listen to the organ play one of your favorite songs."

She managed a giggle. "I won't have a job."

"No problem. This story has a happy ending."

"Okay, go ahead."

"Inside, the church is full of friends and family. On the front pew is Anna, and she's so happy. At the altar, your pastor is smiling and welcoming you to the celebration. Beside him, I'm standing and grinning so big that it looks like my joy has been painted on. I'm about to marry the most beautiful woman in the world." He kissed her forehead. "How do you like my plans?"

"Out of the pages of one of my favorite romance novels."

"Good. I was hoping you'd like the ending. Do we have a date?"

She bit her lip to keep from weeping. "We have a date."

"We need a ring."

"I still have the one you gave me six years ago. It's in my safety deposit box."

He looked startled. "I assumed you'd pawned it or tossed it somewhere." He laughed. "Perfect. Now we have more money for the reception and the honeymoon."

She sighed and allowed herself to dream with him and not think about their circumstances. "I bet Fred and Marta will want to host a reception at their place."

"Barbecue and potato salad?"

She laughed. "I'm sure of it."

"Promise me something." When she nodded, he planted a kiss on her nose. "Tomorrow, or the next day, or the next week, promise me you won't forget how much I love you. God will meet our needs and help us through whatever the future holds."

"I promise."

"I love you, Alina."

"And I love you."

He kissed her, his lips warm and inviting. Oh, what she'd missed these past six years.

"Neon has offered me a vice presidency in Columbus," he said. "I figured it would take us about an hour and a half to visit Anna."

She gasped. "Have you given the position much thought?"

"Some. Honestly not much until tonight. My parents would be doing cartwheels at the thought of me working in the city. I'm wondering if the offer is a blessing. A married man doesn't need to be on the road for weeks at a time."

"Such a delicious prospect. Would you like the work?"

"I'd be a liaison between the smaller cable companies and the executive board. I certainly have the experience, and I'm aware of the needs and challenges existing between the larger and smaller companies."

"Sounds like you're the man for the job, as long as you'd be happy doing it."

"No questions or arguments?"

She wiggled her shoulders. "Nope. Will you need a secretary?"

"Can't do. Neon has strict policies about married people working in the same office."

"Oh, I'm sure I'll find work, and I have a few nibbles on my résumé."

"You don't have to work unless you want to."

"I've held a job since I was fourteen."

"Just think about it." His shoulders lifted and fell. "What about your friend Frank?"

"Frank?" His concern brought more laughter than she'd experienced in a long time.

Ryan frowned. "What is so funny?"

She squeezed his hand. "Frank is Fred's uncle. He's in a nursing home not far from Anna's home. I often have dinner with him on Saturday evenings on the way back from Anna's. I bring him homemade cookies, and he sends me flowers. He's ninety-three."

"Ninety-three?" Ryan grimaced. "Guess I don't have any real competition, then." He planted a kiss on the tip of her nose.

Alina studied the concrete step. Water flowed up the third one, extinguishing the remains of the candle. For now the thunder had ceased. Her fears of the water. . .swimming. . . electrical storms. . .all took form in a nasty demon stabbing at her heart. She took a deep breath bathed in a heavy dose of prayer.

"We need to move to the roof, sweetheart." Ryan released her hand and wrapped his arm around her shoulders.

She could do this. She could do this.

twenty-three

With the northern wind blowing the rain, Ryan doubted an umbrella would shelter them. The extra articles of clothing did little to keep out the torrents of rain. Within minutes Alina and Ryan were soaked. He took a quick glimpse at the light sticks on opposite ends of the roof. In less than an hour, dawn would sweep across the sky like a banner.

"How long do we have?" Alina asked. "I mean, before the water here rises from below us."

"Hard to tell." The truth still ebbed on time and the hope of rescue at sunrise. A deafening waterfall pounded in his ears. He stood in ankle-deep water. In the distance, lightning flashed across the sky. He'd soon have a hysterical Alina on his hands.

"I love you," she said over the drumming weather.

"I love you," he said. "What are we going to name our firstborn?"

"I'm not playing any more games, Ryan. The water is rising faster than before, and another electrical storm is moving this way. This is it. I'm sorry for all the pain I've caused you."

He wanted to shake her, tell her God hadn't abandoned them. Instead he wrapped his arms around her trembling body and kissed her soundly. Releasing her, he stepped to the middle of the roof and raised his hands to the dark sky.

"Lord, we need You. I believe You can save us from this water. Send a helicopter to rescue us."

He glanced back at Alina, and a feeling of warmth surged through his body as though he stood in front of a roaring fire. "We *will* be all right," he said. "I feel it in my spirit."

She shook her head. "I give up, Ryan. I'm sorry, but I can't hope any longer."

For the next thirty minutes, water swarmed the rooftop like the enemy climbing over a fortress. The water rose just below his knees. He didn't want to think about the current washing them away. There was nothing left to hold on to. Alina clung to him, and they watched the eastern sky.

"Do you hear it?" she asked.

His ears perked up. He wanted to believe he heard the sound of a helicopter's rotor blades beating against the wind. "We're here," he shouted. "We're here." The flapping grew closer. "There it is." He waved his arms and shouted again.

Within a few minutes the helicopter hovered over them. "Are you all right?" a man called out over a loudspeaker.

Ryan and Alina nodded, and Ryan gave a thumbs-up sign, knowing the rescuers couldn't hear what was said.

"We'll drop a ladder and get you out of there. Ryan, this is James."

James, the foreman who wanted to break my nose? "Sure glad you found us," Ryan said once he and Alina had climbed safely inside the helicopter.

James laughed above the whirl of the helicopter blades. "Got a guilty conscience over what I'd said to you. Went to apologize at your hotel and couldn't find you. Alina wasn't home either. The more I thought about it, the more I realized you two were still here at Flash. Talked to Fred, and he agreed. Guess you'd say God got my attention."

Alina shook off the wet coat over her head. "You are the best sight I've ever seen."

Ryan drew Alina into his arms. "Look at the sky." Just over the horizon, a trace of dawn in orange and yellow inched its way upward.

"Thank You, Jesus," she sobbed. "Thank You."

"Soon we'll be dry," Ryan said above the roar of the helicopter. "I meant all I said. I love you, and I want us to be married." He peered into her rain-streaked face. "You are beautiful."

"Any man who says I'm beautiful *this* morning has to love me. Do we still have a date in June?"

"Rain or shine."

≈

Saturday, June 11, 12:15 p.m.

The gray clouds that had rolled across the sky all morning with their silent threats of rain dissipated when the courthouse clock chimed the noon hour. In their wake, a veil of blue encircled the small church and sprinkled the day with crystalline sunshine.

Alina lifted her pen from her journal. Since the rescue from the flood, she'd begun to journal a little each day. Ryan encouraged it, and the whole process of putting her thoughts into words was helping to mend the brokenness in her life. She reread her first two sentences for the day and giggled. *I'd never make it as a professional writer.* No matter, this was her wedding day, and she could be as poetic and silly as she wanted.

"Alina, it's a quarter past noon, and the photographer wants one more shot before the ceremony," Deidre said. A crinkle deepened across her forehead.

"Why the frown?" Alina asked. "This is a beautiful day for a wedding, and my matron of honor is somewhere between stressed and full-blown panicked."

"I know. I'm sorry. It's just that I want everything to be perfect." Deidre paced the floor, her small frame draped in pale lavender, looking like a miniature model.

"It doesn't matter if it snows for the wedding. I'm marrying the only man I ever loved, and God has blessed the day."

"I'm so happy for you." Deidre's eyes pooled. "You are breathtaking."

"Don't you dare cry." Alina stiffened and swallowed hard. "Or I will, too." She listened to the stringed instruments in the sanctuary. "I never thought I'd see my wedding day."

"God certainly grabbed your and Ryan's attention," Deidre said. "Thinking about you two nearly drowning on that roof still gives me the shivers."

"Me, too. But it forced Ryan and me to see we were meant to be together." Alina tilted her head. "It also forced us to forgive ourselves for the past."

A knock at the door seized their attention. "Alina, are you about ready?"

She flung open the door to a thinner and healthier Fred. The transition from Flash Communications to Neon Interchange had gone smoothly despite the flood, and the new management was doing an outstanding job as far as Fred was concerned.

"Wow, Marta had better tie you down. You look rather dashing in a tux, young man."

Beaming, Fred grasped his lapels and rocked on his heels. "Yep, I still have what it takes." A grin tugged at his lips. "You *are* gorgeous. Ryan will be too tongue-tied to say his vows."

"He'd better not. I might have to repeat them for him."

"She would, too." Deidre crossed her arms.

Alina took a deep breath and scooped up her bouquet of red and white roses. "Has anyone arrived yet?"

"Well, Ryan and the preacher are here." Fred chuckled. "Those are the two most important ones. And Miss Anna is sitting on the front pew with a woman from Homeward Hills."

"Are the groomsmen and ushers here?"

"Of course. James has been giving the other ushers instructions on which side of the church is for the bride and which side is for the groom. He is so proud of little Jenna being your flower girl."

"I never dreamed James and Ryan would make peace, and now James is directing the ushers." Alina swallowed against the rising emotion. "Takes a big man to admit he's wrong. When we climbed up into that helicopter, James couldn't get his apology out fast enough."

"I appreciated his help after the water went down, although the insurance company took care of it all," Fred said.

"Life has a way of working out when we least expect it," Alina said. "I'm looking forward to chapter two."

A Letter To Our Readers

Dear Reader:

In order that we might better contribute to your reading enjoyment, we would appreciate your taking a few minutes to respond to the following questions. We welcome your comments and read each form and letter we receive. When completed, please return to the following:

Fiction Editor
Heartsong Presents
PO Box 721
Uhrichsville, Ohio 44683

1. Did you enjoy reading *Flash Flood* by DiAnn Mills?
   ❑ Very much! I would like to see more books by this author!
   ❑ Moderately. I would have enjoyed it more if

   _____

   _____

   _____

2. Are you a member of **Heartsong Presents**? ❑ Yes ❑ No
   If no, where did you purchase this book? _____

   _____

3. How would you rate, on a scale from 1 (poor) to 5 (superior), the cover design? _____

4. On a scale from 1 (poor) to 10 (superior), please rate the following elements.

   ____ Heroine   ____ Plot
   ____ Hero   ____ Inspirational theme
   ____ Setting   ____ Secondary characters

5. These characters were special because _____

_____

_____

6. How has this book inspired your life? _____

_____

_____

7. What settings would you like to see covered in future
   Heartsong Presents books? _____

_____

_____

8. What are some inspirational themes you would like to see
   treated in future books? _____

_____

_____

9. Would you be interested in reading other **Heartsong
   Presents** titles? ❑ Yes   ❑ No

10.   Please check your age range:
      ❑ Under 18   ❑ 18-24
      ❑ 25-34   ❑ 35-45
      ❑ 46-55   ❑ Over 55

Name _____

Occupation _____

Address _____

City, State, Zip _____

fresh-brewed love

4 stories in 1

Four women find grounds for love where romance blossoms over cups of coffee. Can these women make the right decisions when it comes to love? Authors include Susan K. Downs, Anita Higman, DiAnn Mills, and Kathleen Y'Barbo.

Contemporary, paperback,
352 pages, 5³/₁₆" x 8"

_____